I0780669

Memories & Revelations

A Collection of Stories

Compiled by Lisa Bell

RADICAL WOMEN

Scripture quotations marked with (KJV) are from The Authorized (King James) Version. Rights in the Authorized Version in the United Kingdom are vested in the Crown. Reproduced by permission of the Crown's patentee, Cambridge University Press

Scripture quotations marked as (NAS) are taken from the (NASB®) New American Standard Bible®, Copyright © 1960, 1971, 1977, 1995, 2020 by The Lockman Foundation. Used by permission. All rights reserved. lockman.org

Scripture quotations marked (NIV) are taken from The Holy Bible, New International Version®, NIV®. Copyright © 1973, 1978, 1984, 2011 by Biblica, Inc. Used with permission of Zondervan. All rights reserved worldwide. www.zondervan.com

Scripture marked (NKJV) are taken from the New King James Version®. Copyright © 1982 by Thomas Nelson. Used by permission. All rights reserved.

Scripture quotations marked (NLT) are taken from the Holy Bible, New Living Translation, copyright ©1996, 2004, 2015 by Tyndale House Foundation. Used by permission of Tyndale House Publishers, Carol Stream, Illinois 60188. All rights reserved.

Scripture quotations marked (RSV) are from the Revised Standard Version of the Bible, Copyright © 1946, 1952, and 1971 the Division of Christian Education of the National Council of te Churches of Christ in the United States of America. Used by permission. All rights reserved.

Scripture marked (TLV) are taken from the Holy Scriptures, Tree of Life Version*. Copyright © 2014,2016 by the Tree of Life Bible Society. Used by permission of the Tree of Life Bible Society.

Copyright © 2025 by Radical Women

All rights reserved.

No portion of this book may be reproduced in any form without written permission from the publisher or author, except as permitted by U.S. copyright law. Authors contributing to this work retain the copyright for individual submissions but not to the work as a whole. True stories in the work come from the perspective of the author. Names and places may have been changed to protect the innocent (or guilty). Entries marked with * are fictional accounts. Any resemblance to persons living or dead is purely coincidental.

Paperback ISBN: 978-1-965561-11-9
eBook ISBN: 978-1-965561-12-6
Special edition Hardcover ISBN: 978-1-965561-13-3

COPYRIGHT

To writers and aspiring writers,
keep creating, keep writing,
and pursue publication
with the passion your dreams deserve.

Contents

Acknowledgments

Thank you to all the authors who contributed to this collection of stories (both true and fictional), poetry, photos, and inspirational pieces. Without your work, this book wouldn't exist. And thank you to the families who allow authors to write, even when it sometimes takes time from you. Your continued support enables them to pursue the call God placed on their lives. I pray each author pursues the path to continue writing and publishing.

Thank you to The Heights Church in Granbury and to Roaring Lambs/Roaring Writers for small groups that provide feedback and encouragement to those who desire improvements in writing and making their way toward publication. Continued support of these organizations provide the structure that make small groups of writers successful. I can't wait to see what God does with these two groups that fuel me and acknowledge my gifts, talents, and calling.

To Christine and Amber who gave me a second set of eyes during editing. Thank you Dee Dee for heading up a committee for a launch party and Amber for managing the online launch when the time comes. It's easy to think I can do this alone, but knowing I could doesn't mean I should. A team helps when working on a project such as this.

Above all, thank You our Lord, Jesus Christ. For without You, our writings might entertain but would never change a life. We give You all glory and honor for this publication and whatever success we see from it. May those who read it draw closer to You or come to You for the first time. You remind us daily of where we walked before and what we learned from those memories. Remind our readers of the times when You showed up and showed out for them, too.

Lisa Bell
Radical Women

Welcome to Our World

Lisa Bell

The world of a writer encompasses hours of time spent alone, planning, plotting, thinking, and finally crafting a story readers enjoy. While few take on a project sitting in a room with other writers, many times we need such an environment to brainstorm ideas. We crave time with other writers.

Writing groups breathe life into authors. Without the camaraderie, feedback, and encouragement, I suspect many of us might quit before we ever finish any serious project. In our groups, we learn skills and perfect our styles, but we also share ideas—no matter how crazy they seem.

As a leader of multiple groups, I went to one of our weekly meetings during the fall of 2024.

A member piped up. "We should do an anthology. It would give everyone a chance to be published."

I have stories in anthologies—one or two of which I admit investing time to help develop. While I nodded in agreement, part of me shuddered. Anthologies can take a lot of time—especially if you're the one compiling the work.

Maybe the three groups' members wouldn't agree. Maybe they didn't want to take part in an anthology. And maybe I could get away with dismissing the idea with a smile.

Yeah, right.

Not.

Most of the members in all three of my groups loved the idea. And I invited a few from outside those groups to jump on board. We chose a theme—because an anthology needs some sense of coherence. We have an eclectic bunch of writers in these groups. Writers of poetry, fiction, and nonfiction, both traditional authors and independent-published ones. Then we have newer writers who started their journeys less than a year ago. Some more advanced than others, but all with a dream to see their names in a published book—and not only on an acknowledgments page. Some enjoy photography, willing to add pictures to enhance our book baby.

Thus, *Memories & Revelations* became a thing.

Because many of these writers haven't gone through the process of seeking publication, they got a taste of the process. After sending an online query, they signed an agreement and submitted their works. Yes, I can be harsh as a leader when necessary. No one complained, although we had a few bumps along the way trying to deal with technology.

Anthologies provide authors a chance to see publication before they finish a book project. But they also benefit our beloved readers. When you pick up an anthology, you get a variety of styles. In this instance, you also get a smattering of genres. But each piece of work meets the criteria of a memory where God showed the author something—a revelation that transformed them. Even the short stories in this collection originated with a memory. After all, most fiction has a basis in personal lives.

Enjoy these offerings, and may they remind you of a time when God taught you something deeper than you expected from an ordinary event or moment.

If you like the style of one writer, be sure to find him or her on social media and follow so you stay updated on any future releases.

Sight

Madison Whiteaker

When you lose your sight,
The LORD is your might.
He will make you see.
Then hell will plea.
It will cry out,
Or maybe even pout.
Then the trumpets will play,
And you shall pray.
For the LORD is your sight,
And he gives you might!

Crashing Waves

Lisa Bell

Copyright 2023 Lisa Bell

Puddles and Mama's Little Layer Cake

Becky Kubiak

As I see it, the best part of Christmas is all the food. Turkey, mashed potatoes, gravy, bacon in the green beans, rolls. I drool just thinking about it. And then, the "coup de gras" is the awesome MAMA'S LITTLE LAYER CAKE. It is the favorite of the family, originally made by Mom's great-grandmother, Mama. Everyone loves it, but no one has ever saved me a piece or even let me clean their plate. Mom only makes this cake a few times a year since it takes six to eight hours to finish.

After 17 years of being a good boy, I think it is high time I get my piece of this secret family recipe. So you understand, it is 16 luscious layers of the best cake you ever put in your mouth. When the layers are ready to assemble, they are stacked together with alternating soft, yummy fudge between each cake layer, fudge drizzling down the side. Even with 16 layers, it stands only eight or nine inches tall. No one passes up the chance to eat this cake. I have watched the strongest-willed dieting family members fight to lick the cake plate!

Since I am only 12 pounds, they could share. Right? It is not like I'm going to get fat!

Mom plans to make THE CAKE today, so I am plotting the heist of at least one piece.

First, I need to figure out how to do this.

"Hmmm, distraction might work."

Mom is a sucker for my love and attention. I wag my tail, look up into her eyes, and she melts. She loves my kisses and will sit and hold me anytime I want her to. She loves me so much that when I caught the house on fire, she didn't even get mad. I almost died from embarrassment when the fireman flipped me over, pointed to my manly parts, and said that caused the fire. How was I to know peeing on the VCR would make a spark that turned into a fire?

So, as you can imagine, I don't want that kind of distraction again. I will show her how much I love her. She'll melt! I always try to be there for her, especially if she has a bad day. I know, in spite of everything, I am her favorite.

But a few days ago, I had a terrible thing happen. My back legs went out, and all l could do was drag my body to her. She picked me up, gave me meds, and gently held me until the meds kicked in. I heard her talking to Dad, and he said the next time I threw my back out, they should put me out of my misery—whatever that means.

Now, back to my plan. Today is not a great day. But I don't have the luxury of picking the day to bake. My back hurts a little, so I pull myself to the doorway. Mom has tears in her eyes and tells me how much she loves me. She gives me a fuzzy blanket. Nice, but she missed my point. I just wanted to remind her I was here to help make the cake. With sad eyes, she got out the eggs, flour, sugar, vanilla, and butter. I watched every move. If she would just leave the room for even a minute, I could taste the cake batter she is mixing. (But of course she doesn't leave.)

Still getting ready to bake, she first butters the cake pans. I LOVE butter! She glanced at me every so often with that sad smile. She seems so forlorn, but I don't know why. Usually, this is a fun thing. When she starts baking the cakes, four layers at a time, I know. I am not going to get the butter or the batter, so I move out of the way. With a deep sigh, I lower my old bones onto the blanket in the hallway. Maybe I'll close my eyes for a minute, but I doubt it. I was on full alert the entire time.

Mom has a pattern for getting the layers done. Butter, batter, and then the oven. As soon as the cakes are ready to take out of the oven, she lets them cool in the pan for just a few minutes and then carefully lifts the very thin layer out of the pan and places it on wax paper to cool completely. Each layer is spread out on the dining room table. She washes the pan, butters it, and off we go with another layer. The same routine always, until all the batter is cooked and cooled.

About the time she took out the last layer, I had a "light bulb" moment! Pretend I can't walk. She will feel so sorry for me she will leave the cakes alone on the table (all 16 layers) while she takes care of me.

I drag my almost limp body into the kitchen; a little yelp here and there for effect. She gets that stricken look on her face, picks me up, and calls Dad. Crying, she explains what has happened. She begs him to come home because she needs him and can't do IT alone. He assures her I will be okay for the few minutes it will take for him to get there. Then, they can go to the vet's office together and do what has to be done.

She gently lays me on the blanket. Sobbing, she heads up the stairs to change. I try to follow her, but I can't pull myself up even one step. As I turn around, I happen to notice the dining room chair pulled away from the table. I can do it! Now or never. The chance of my lifetime. I will give it my best!

And just as she comes down the stairs and Dad bursts through the front door, they catch me red-pawed. I am standing in the middle of the table with crumbs falling off my lips, a huge smile on my face, my tail wagging as fast as it could go. I ate a bite from each of the 16 layers.

In my defense; I am old and probably feeble-minded (wink)! But it was worth it.

Details

Mary-margaret Belota

I remember every detail,
every single, solitary,
teeny, tiny detail,
from the nods in the Fine Arts lounge
to the concord in court,
I can't remember what I had for supper last night
or where I put my glasses,
but I remember every detail
of our time together.

I remember how desperately I loved you.
I was desperate to be with you,
desperate to convince you of my love,
desperate to love away your wounds.
At nineteen
I actually believed that was possible.

And I was desperate for freedoms only imagined
until you gave them substance.
I remember every detail.

Sometimes it is as if the entirety of our life together
is blasted into my brain
in one instantaneous download—
the whole of our 25 years
in one panoramic burst
of breathtaking clarity
all these years later.

And standing in the waterfall of memory,
the only prayer from my lips
is gratitude,
because for every crippling action,
there was an opposite
and equally empowering reaction.

And in the final distillation,
there is no pain to be conjured,
no hurt to be unearthed,
no unforgiveness to be exorcised.
I remember every detail.

I have absolute,
inviolable,
incontrovertible
selective recall.

I remember every detail,
of the details I choose to remember.[1]

---

1. Belota, M.-m. (2022). *Moving Forward, A Journey to Letting Go.* Screened Porch
Publishing.

Fleeing to Safety in God's Arms

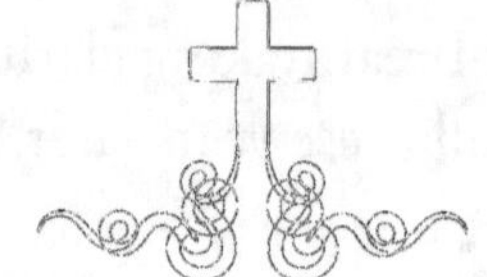

Barbara Boothe Loyd

I fainted after the airline clerk looked at me and said, "I'm so sorry. There is a problem with your tickets."

The startled man standing in line behind me grunted as he partially broke my fall before my head hit the terrazzo floor.

My mother had come to Germany from the States for a visit. I hoped to fly home with her before my husband found out the children and I would not return. After I became conscious again, Mother offered me a sip of Coke. I gathered my composure and stood in line again. When it was my turn, the clerk apologized for giving me such a fright earlier. She explained the children and I could fly as scheduled, but we could not be on the same flight as my mother. At last, thankful and relieved, I held our three tickets securely in my hands and waved them to my smiling mother.

My fainting, triggered by fear of being unable to leave my abusive husband, revealed the tense emotional state I remained in while planning our escape.

My co-Sunday School teacher who worked in the Army's Judge Advocate General's office told me, "Abusers get worse, not better, and I urge you to leave your husband as soon as possible."

"Daddy does mean things to Mommy." Amy and Clyde told their grandmother of their concerns when they stayed in her room at our rented house in Germany. After my husband left for an inspection for the Army, my mother questioned me at breakfast about the children's comments. Relieved finally to tell the truth, I no longer covered up his cruel, abusive bullying of me and the children.

A few weeks before our escape, I had one last appointment at the Army's dermatology clinic. It turned out to be the culminating event that convinced me to leave. During the time I sought relief from a strange skin condition, I never saw the same doctor twice. The skin on my hands sloughed off in sheets. Different doctors on call during those months had prescribed various creams and bandages. However, this doctor looked back through all my treatment records. He noticed that in nine months my condition was worsening rather than healing.

He looked at me and said, "You must make a very hard emotional decision if you want to overcome this condition."

Without telling the doctor about my home situation, I resolved to follow through with my plan to start a new life. As I walked along the corridors of the hospital, back to my car, I felt sure that God had spoken through this doctor. The handwriting on the walls of my heart flashed in neon letters. YOU NEED TO LEAVE YOUR TORMENTOR.

During her visit, Mother also said, "You know you must leave him."

I recognized this truth but was not sure how to flee safely. If Reggie suspected we would not return from the States, I feared he would keep the children with him.

Finally, I made my husband a promise. "The children and I will visit with your parents and other family members while we're in the States."

He thought that was a good idea. The following day, I taped a large cardboard box together and filled it with the children's clothes. Underneath their duds, I put in my family silver, the only valuable thing I packed.

I prayed for protection and reassurance of God's presence in my plan. A few days after I secured our plane tickets, my husband drove us to the Frankfurt airport many miles from our house. The trip went well. After we arrived at the airport, our farewells to Reggie were said, hugs were exchanged, then my children and I walked onto our plane. My legs shook as we boarded and found our seats. My mother's plane left about thirty minutes later than our flight. We looked forward to our rendezvous at LaGuardia Airport in New York. The children were excited about the airplane trip but soon went to sleep. My prayers were constant.

Nine hours later we arrived in New York, connected with Mother, caught our plane to New Orleans, and rented a car, which I drove to her place in Baton Rouge. With the time change and hours of travel, I had been awake for over twenty-four hours. After the long journey, we all slept well.

When we awoke, the movie *Yankee Doodle Dandy*, starring Jimmy Cagney, was on Mother's television. Later, the 4th of July celebrations televised on PBS reminded me how much I missed them while living in Germany. Amy was six and a half and Clyde was five—perfect ages to appreciate the fireworks and to enjoy hearing English spoken on television. Jet lag captured us again, and we enjoyed deep slumber the second night home.

Mother returned to work the following week. I made phone calls and learned that in Louisiana it takes a minimum of a year to obtain a divorce.

When I telephoned my sister, she urged me, "Come to Houston to be near us; your kids will have cousins to play with."

Bettye, my older sister, always acted like a mother hen to me and our younger brother. My faith in her good judgment never diminished.

She continued, "You know John would love to have Amy and Clyde attend his school. Think of the fun those three children can have. A divorce in Texas doesn't take as long as in Louisiana."

I prayed and considered our situation for a couple of days before I bought three tickets for the Greyhound Bus ride to Texas. The trip became an exciting adventure for the children. Bettye and her six-year-old son, John, met us at the depot in downtown Houston. My kids jumped up and down when they saw their cousin. I felt bolstered by Bettye's practical nature as we drove back to their house in Sugar Land.

The kids enjoyed a slumber party with John and his two older siblings while I fell into a deep slumber in the guest room. The following morning, my sister suggested I talk to a friend of hers, an attorney. I agreed. She made the appointment and drove me to his office.

Before we went inside, Bettye assured me, "Logene and his wife have been our friends for years. He will give you good legal advice."

While we sat in his office, he outlined the steps necessary to file for divorce in Texas.

Before we left, he asked me, "Would you consider taking a job here as my legal secretary?"

I hesitated a bit then said, "Yes."

I thought, *since I haven't worked in a while, the typing skills I learned in high school will be useful after all.*

Next, Bettye and her husband, Leon, contacted their friends who had a car for sale. It was a silver Pontiac with a black roof. After I bought it, the kids and I named it "Gray Goose." A day later, Bettye contacted a woman in her historical society who owned rental properties. She had a vacant house available in Sugar Land, which we drove by to view. I had managed to squirrel away a few hundred dollars before leaving Germany, which was a miracle because my husband made me account for every cent. I paid the first month's rent when I signed the lease for the house. I was overjoyed to hear that the elementary school bus stopped in front of the house.

After eating dinner that evening, I composed a letter to my husband's commanding officer in Germany, which explained our current situation. I asked him to assist by ordering the release of household furniture stored with the Army in San Antonio before we moved to Germany. A few days after we moved into the rented house, the furniture arrived. By the time school began in August, the children had new playmates whose mother kept them after school to play with her three children until I returned home from work.

The bravest thing I ever undertook, with God's help, was to move forward with the escape plan. Once I made up my mind, it was the most significant day of my life.

A week after we arrived at my sister's house, I awoke one morning and noticed my hands' new, smooth skin. I praised God for this miracle of healing. Our new, peaceful environment and the assurance of feeling Him at work in the details for our future allowed my hands to heal.

Mom's Legacy—Rich or Poor

Adalia (Dee Dee) Ward

Mom graduated from the 11th grade in Corsicana, Texas before relocating to San Antonio, Texas. Work became mandatory. She would not have more school ahead of her. She rushed, deciding to marry Dad, the milkman. This marriage did not fulfill her aspirations for a powerful, self-reliant, and protective husband, who might improve her status and provide well for her. Dad, uneducated with low self-esteem, but tall, dark, and handsome.

The narrative continued with innocent love, insufficient resources, poor compensation, and a tough existence.

Then came baby one.

Then baby two.

Baby three.

And finally, baby me.

November 1950. As the last child my parents planned, Mom had her tubes tied while at the hospital, after bringing me into the world. The fourth child, the second girl, with two older brothers to greet me. Mom named me Adalia without Dad's approval, because Dad called me Judy until the day he died at 87. Mom murmured after the siblings could not come close to pronouncing my name. "Call her Dee Dee. That will work."

Mom's quick decision to solve the problem with my name proved to be a blessing. She resolved issues, always rolling that way!

We did not have a phone. It never became a necessity. Our neighbor, Mrs. Barnes, allowed Mom to receive and place calls from her phone. She screened the calls and never bothered Mom with the bill collectors. She stood on her front porch and yelled out toward our front porch. My sister and I cleaned Mrs. Barnes' house on Friday afternoons to repay her kindness.

Our lack of money became clear to me the summer before my seventh-grade year. To pay for our school clothes, Mom and Dad said we must pick up pecans to sell. Mom loaded up a delicious picnic lunch with blankets, plenty of sweet Kool-Aid, fried chicken, cornbread, and a cold, red watermelon.

Dad prevented us from playing. "These are workdays, kiddos. Let's buy some school clothes. Here are your buckets. Get to work."

We needed new shoes, clothes, and school supplies. The four of us were growing like weeds, and the pressure to provide for us fell on my mother's shoulders. She cried, visibly and audibly, when she was unable to fulfill our wants.

Mom bragged about us and our exuberant energy. As the day progressed, she snuck in hugs and praises. Amid the lush pastures of huge, mature pecan trees, breathing in the fresh air was so freeing. This supplied us with hundreds of fruits to fulfill our dreams of new clothes.

We regretted leaving the vast mesmerizing fields as Mom sang "Que Sera, Sera."

Dad loaded the truck and complained about the number of buckets that weren't quite full. The cost of four kids lingered over his head. If he sold that day, would he need to return the next for more?

Dad mumbled as he rolled a Prince Albert cigarette and glanced over at Mom while she straightened her pedal pushers to roll down the curvy calves on her petite legs.

Mom glanced across the truck bed at Dad's dark-tanned face. "How much per pound should we expect to get for these paper-shell pecans?"

Dad never answered. Mom did not persist in getting the answer.

We were aware of the weakness our dad portrayed because of his inability to assist our mom in stretching the meager money flowing into our household. He retreated with a desire to be alone if a conversation about our lack of funds arose. His six-foot-three-inch stature would hunch over, with rounded shoulders, as he felt powerless with mental fatigue. Eyes blank, head shaking, he drifted off toward the chicken pens in the backyard. Weeks without income were a consequence of his seasonal employment. The cotton gin, ice icehouse, peach orchards—all jobs he counted on for work—left our family with inconsistent paydays. Never enough.

We never doubted Mom and Dad's love for each other. The hugs and kisses came frequently and mushy.

Mom saved us and our screams by shouting, "Don't look!"

She pushed us to present our family in an approving social manner. But Dad, despite coming from a much more dignified family than my mom's drunken background, did not observe any rules or regulations.

Mother held us all together, and she yearned for a better life for us. Mom emphasized the importance of being thankful for our delicious hot food on our table.

She said, "I starved to death when Dad and I lived with his parents. A one-bite vanilla wafer cookie got cut in half for my dessert. Let's be grateful to the Lord for our provisions."

She ensured Dad was sitting at the table and heard her comments.

Life progressed through the years. Mom shouldered the stress of a large family with limited resources. Mom's Uncle Adolf always saved us from disparity. He drove a station wagon, slung low to the ground, and loaded with tools and leftover repair materials. He always wore blue denim overalls and paint-stained shoes. His gray hair flowed in long curls from beneath his sweat-stained straw hat.

We were fortunate to live in a small house he built years earlier, paying a modest rent of $25 a month. This home was in a pleasant neighborhood. He often came by and dropped off bushels of peaches, sweet potatoes, or anything he knew we would appreciate. We always rushed to his car to greet him, knowing he never came without goodies.

It appeared Mom was his favorite for this type of arrangement. Plus, he always came to her defense. "Take care of your mom. She is a jewel."

We received blessings and learned to pray as the years passed. All four kids kneeled around our mom, circling her with grateful smiles, spilling over with laughter and goofy remarks. Squeaky-clean faces gazed into her warm hazel eyes; her hair pulled back away from her face as she filled us full of Bible stories and reasons for us to thank our Lord above.

"Jesus loves me. Yes, I know..."

In my junior year of high school, another reminder of our financial difficulties surfaced. Oh goodness. Chris, a tall, smart president of the student council, asked me to the prom. He awaited my answer, trembling before my outburst.

Could I? Should I?

"Yes."

His dad was the president of the local college, and he planned to be one of the adult chaperones at the prom.

How could I, a girl like me, overcome this challenge?

With nervous hands, a cold sweat broke out on my forehead as I presented my dilemma to Mom.

"Oh, Mom. I don't have to go. I could get sick. That could happen."

Helplessness grew like a burning fire in my stomach. Hope was disappearing. Tears formed in the corners of my inexperienced eyes.

"Mom, should I dream of going to the prom? I understand if I can't."

"Do you like this, boy? Do you want to go?"

"I do, Mom."

My sweet mother knew how to manage the issue of preparing me. She never worried me with her concern but kept me eager and confident. Mom whistled and danced me around the room. Dad whirled me first with my bare feet on his and then glided me in a slow process as "Blue Velvet" played on the record player. He showed me how to handle myself on a dance floor.

"Move slow. Feel the music and let him lead you."

They enjoyed themselves.

Would this have a favorable outcome? Should I believe? Should I dream?

Mom and Dad sometimes tucked us kids into bed and enjoyed some private time dancing in the kitchen on the old black-and-white linoleum floor. They shoved the chrome dining set with six chairs toward the warm, worn-wood cabinets. Two unattended cigarettes, close together in an amber glass ashtray, and burning down, created a dreadful smoky atmosphere in the room. We could hear them giggling, their feet sliding, and country music playing. Dad assumed the flirty part, and Mom always wore her red lipstick for him. As we listened, the atmosphere filled with peace and affection.

The next morning, Phil, the third-born child, my favorite brother, groaned and moaned the loudest upon seeing Baby Ruth wrappers in the kitchen trash. Daddy's favorite candy bar. Two Coke-a-Cola empty glass bottles sat on the back porch.

"What? A party without the kids?"

As I grew older, I reflected and realized Mom arranged these occurrences to be the glue to keep them connected through the strenuous days they endured.

Upon returning home from school two days before the prom, my miracle materializes in my closet. A beautiful, modest, shiny, white, some kind of satin, long dress appeared. Mom never explained how—only why.

"I can't explain, Dee Dee. You will understand when you become a mom."

"I love it, Mom!" I could smell the newness. Only then did I believe. "I am going to the prom."

Later that evening, my brother, Phil, pulled a seven-dollar price tag from the trash, along with a layaway payment ticket. We never told Mom. To me, this dress was priceless.

Prom night came, and Mom pulled my shoulder-length, dishwater-blond hair into a bouffant bubble. From somewhere appeared a pair of white satin shoes, pearl clamp-on earrings, and a snow-white fake-fur wrap. Mom summoned some favors. I didn't see those items again after prom night. She borrowed and later returned those items.

I hugged Mom. My heartfelt tears flowed, and she whispered, "Don't cry. You are beautiful. You have become a porcelain princess with reddish-pink lipstick and a gleam in your eyes. Go have fun!"

As I looked in the gold-framed floor-length mirror in Mom's bedroom, I knew my miracle had come true. I pulled my shoulders back. Confidence overtook the smile on my face.

Chris smiled from ear-to-ear during the introduction to his father. I swayed back and forth with the music and held my prom date's hand with pride. We both stood tall during the photo taking, as I remained under the spell of his cologne. What a wonderful memory that remained a lifetime.

Mom waited up for me. She showed her delight with the smile on my face.

"I fit right in with the other girls, Mom. Chris and I danced amazingly together."

Was I poor? Not that night. And not anymore.

"I love you, Mom! Without your resourcefulness, I know the prom would not have been possible. I hope to be a mother just like you someday."

Mom stayed strong in her faith in God. Her faith grabbed hold of what grace made available. Her wisdom educated me and stayed with me forever.

A godly mother's legacy blessed me with abundant riches.

Never again did I experience being poor.

Mom's Legacy—Rich or Poor (Poem)

Adalia (Dee Dee) Ward

How does a child know
if they are rich or poor?
Receiving gifts or necessities
with smiles and hugs.
How does a child know
if they are rich or poor?
Receiving gifts or necessities
with moans and groans.
How does a child know
By the count of the items?
Or the price tags?
Or the required thank you?

A child knows,
if he or she is taught
by lessons of faith and grace.
By wise mothers
performing miracles through God.

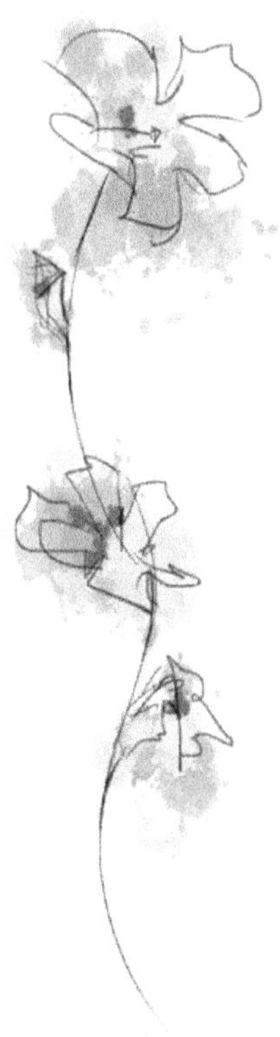

Destiny of a Name

Amber Whiteaker

Chestnut lashes lay on soft chubby cheeks as I waited for that ideal moment to transfer him into his crib. His first Christmas was around the corner, and my thoughts wandered to future traditions we'd make and gifts to purchase. The rest of the world launched full force into the busyness of the season. But I found mine slowing as it drifted to a night, over two millennia prior, when another mother gazed on the mahogany hairs resting on the rounded apples under her Son's sleepy lids. Only months before, the messenger prophesied of His destiny. The journey He would walk mattered—not only for their people, but for the entirety of humanity. She knew her desires for marriage and grandchildren would never come to fruition through her firstborn. How deeply she must have not only loved Him but valued her relationship with His Father to set aside her dreams for His purpose—His Father's plan.

I glanced at the clock hanging on the wall and realized if I didn't shift my snoozing child onto his mattress soon, he would be in my arms for another hour. I would most definitely feel the lack of sleep in the morning. Back in his crib, with his lovey nestled next to the arm that somehow found its way out of the swaddle, I patted his back to soothe him into deeper slumber. I wondered if Mary ever felt overwhelmed with mothering the boy whose destiny affected all humankind from that point forward. Did soothing Him in the wee hours of the morning, while the rest of the household slept, bring her peace or cause her thoughts to wander like mine? His name meant God's salvation. Mine was the son of the valiant warrior—bold destinies for such tiny packages of innocence.

I blinked, and Christmas faded into the new year—twice. My toddler never seemed to lack energy. His stocky bundle of enthusiasm endured from the moment his eyelids sensed the first rays of light at the edge of his blackout curtains until they drooped in exhaustion at the last possible moment of each evening.

One night, not unlike any other during this second year of his life, I ventured into his room to return books to his bookshelf, cars to their soft-sided cube, and his still-wired little self back into his bed. Bedtime routines seemed to make no difference. He slept when his fumes depleted—and not a moment sooner. I heard the familiar creak of his mattress and sighed on my third trek to his room. He was oblivious to my entrance, standing on his bed while swinging an invisible—something—over his head and into the darkness beyond his nightlight. Was he fishing? I gathered him into my arms, whispered gentle reminders in his ear, and tucked him in again. This time, I would sit until he slept. I was tired, even if he wasn't.

Trying to figure out the scene I witnessed proved futile. "Hey, Buddy. What were you doing when I came in?"

"My was fighting Goliath! My was swinging my wocks!" His tiny chest puffed to twice its normal size as a grin stretched from ear-to-ear. One of these days, he would learn proper pronouns—and how to pronounce that pesky "r" sound.

"Oh! I see! Did you show him God's on your side?"

"Yes! God helped my wock knock him down!"

I couldn't resist the upturn of my lips as a little giggle escaped, and I kissed him once more. "I'm so glad, Buddy. It's time for sleeping now. You need your strength to fight tomorrow."

His fingers grasped mine until they grew heavy and slipped to the mattress as his breathing evened out and sleep triumphed. I don't know when my body moved to its prone position on the floor next to his bed, but the vision that flashed through my semi-conscious mind felt surreal. A teenage boy, with my little warrior's chestnut locks and upturned nose, trudged through a battlefield of broken and wounded bodies carrying a sword in each hand—one glistening in the firelight and the other tattered from years of writing its contents on his heart.

I shot up from the floor to reassure myself the little guy still slept in peace there in our two-story townhouse in Minnesota. He wasn't on a battlefield. It wasn't real. But did the name God gave me years before his birth prophesy his future like the name given to Mary? Did she ever startle from sleep after visions of Him on a hill outside their city walls? Did the bleating of the Passover lamb echo in her ears long after rising to face her daily tasks? I could never imagine precisely what she endured. His fate was so much harsher than my son's would ever be. But knowing His future, how did she ever let Him out of her sight? The knowledge of how long it would take me to get my baby boy back to dreamland was all that kept me from plucking him from his bed and clutching him as close to my heart as possible in that moment. Though tears streamed down my face, a strange peace washed over me as a breeze whispered in my ear—I know the plans I have for him, plans for prosperity and not for disaster, plans to give him hope and a future. What is impossible for man is possible with Me.

The clarity of that vision hasn't waned in the decade since it first flashed across my thoughts and embedded itself into my spirit. His hair is longer now, and a couple more years tarry before he reaches teenage status, but little else differs from the young man on that battlefield. His Bible already shows evidence of heavy use. He knows many passages better than I do, especially those narratives of heroes like Joshua, David, and, of course, Jesus. Anxiety occasionally intrudes, but not with the frequency of his early years. As I raise my valiant warrior son, I find comfort in knowing Mary raised hers to pray for him...love him...and provide the ultimate sacrifice for him.

How she let Him go confounds me, but I'll have to do the same. She didn't do it alone, though—and neither will I.

What's Cluttering My Table

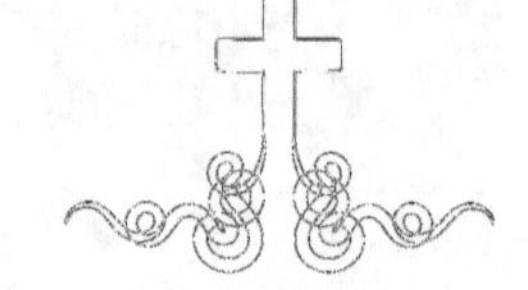

Wanda Strange

January found me running on empty, discouraged, and depleted. I can't blame it on a busy holiday as this season was much less hectic than others in my life. Without energy to engage in my usual activities or take on any additional projects, the new year seemed the perfect time to hibernate.

Over the past couple of years, doctors' visits and medical procedures squeezed an already overcrowded schedule. At the end of the year, it was past time to push the reset button.

God blesses me with many abilities. I can do lots of things. Some of them I do relatively well. I often remind myself of an old adage. "Just because you can, doesn't mean you should."

My personality drives me to be active. I like being busy and engaged. Often, this tendency causes me to take on too much. Perhaps my desire to please and never disappoint anyone causes me to say "yes" when I should say "no." I know better, but somehow, I find myself with too many obligations, too little time and running from one meeting to another and one task to another.

A recent women's retreat focused on coming away and abiding in Jesus. Aha! Dilemma identified. It is impossible to abide anywhere when constantly in motion.

In the Gospel, Martha struggled with the same issue. I identified with Martha, the woman who got things done. She made sure everyone was fed and welcomed in her home. However, instead of enjoying her guests, she grew tired and resentful. She needed help—someone to share the load. More than help, she needed rest and restoration at the feet of Jesus. She implored Jesus to instruct her sister to assist with dinner preparations. Instead, He admonished her.

"Martha, Martha," the Lord answered, "you are worried and upset about many things, but few things are needed—or indeed only one. Mary has chosen what is better, and it will not be taken away from her." (Luke 10:41-42 NIV).

What happened next? Did Martha sit down at Jesus' feet? Did she return to the kitchen and sulk? Did she respond, "But Lord, who's going to feed all these people?"

The Bible left these questions unanswered. I asked myself the same while I rationalized my crowded calendar. I kept pushing myself, not wanting to shirk my responsibilities or let anyone down.

Like Martha, I needed to be still and rest. Would I keep going until an illness or some family crisis forced me to slow down?

Would He say to me, "Wanda, Wanda, you are worried and upset about many things, but few things are really needed—or indeed only one. Choose to come away with me and let me restore you."

I prayed. "Lord, I want to be obedient. Help me slow down before You slow me down."

Clearing my calendar, I entered an intentional season of reflection. I declined invitations. I delegated responsibilities. I physically rested. I sat still and listened for Holy Spirit to speak. I heard little things along the way; sometimes in my personal Bible study, other times in the words of a trusted friend, and often in the words of songs. God lovingly used whatever means necessary to communicate with me. As I listened, Holy Spirit confirmed the message I heard.

One sleepless night, as I watched YouTube, I happened upon a video. Really? I don't believe in coincidences. The message was clearly put there for me to find at exactly the right time. I listened to Anthony Evans as he described a season of life. He could have inserted my name into his story.

Following his mother's death in 2019, Anthony stopped only briefly to mourn his beloved mother. He immersed himself in his gospel music ministry. He continued powering through, touring, and accepting commitments because he didn't want to disappoint anyone. Even while he continued to serve God, he felt empty. In despair, he cried out to God for answers.

Anthony shared God's revelation to his spirit. A childhood memory illustrated a spiritual truth. He remembered his daily routine, spreading homework over the dining room table to work while his mother prepared dinner.

"Anthony, dinner is almost ready. Clear the table. I won't put food on it until you clean it off."

Ouch!

A stab to my heart. My table was so full, I left no room for God to feed me.

I needed to clear the table to make space for Him to provide the feast He prepared for me.

God doesn't want me so busy I don't have time to spend with Him. When He gives me an assignment to serve someone, He wants me to leave time and space on my calendar to meet the need.

I just celebrated my 74th birthday. Realistically, there are a lot more days behind than ahead of me. In this season of life, I want to be obedient and allow God to feed, guide, and continue to use me. I pray to walk with Him, doing the things He leads me to do. As long as I am breathing, He has a purpose for me. I desire to finish strong without a cluttered table.

Singing Off-key at the Homeless Shelter*

Christine Kohler

Carol sang "Away in the Manger" off-key as she eased her Ford Focus into the last spot at the homeless shelter. She turned the wheel to finish parking when the car lurched. A sickening crunch sounded from the back bumper. By the time Carol unfastened her seatbelt and got out of the car, the other driver sped off.

"Great," Carol said to no one. "Merry Christmas to you, too."

She sighed and gathered the contents of her open purse off the floor. Should she call State Farm or her husband first? He wasn't going to be happy with an accident driving up their rates. She checked the time. Late. She'd have to deal with the creased bumper later.

Carol made her way to the front door of the San Antonio Metropolitan Ministries building. As sleet and rain pelted her face, Carol wished she hadn't come. She tried not to think about her husband and children and grandchildren enjoying pecan pie and cookies by a toasty fire and lighted tree without her.

A long line of people snaked down the side of the red brick building, around the corner, and out of sight. Many of the rag-tag band looked as if they'd run out into the night when their houses caught fire. Instead of wearing coats, boots, and scarves, they huddled under dirty blankets, or wore sweaters and sandals. All their worldly possessions were gathered in sacks. For the two years Carol had been working at the shelter, she couldn't get over the magnitude of need.

A cold wind whipped through her hair, and she turned up her coat collar. Carol stared at a veteran wearing an Army jacket and clutching his beggar's sign. She knew firsthand the frustration of patients-rights laws that kept family members from forcing the mentally ill to seek help. Still, where were their families? For pity sakes, it was Christmas Eve!

The guard at the front door eyed Carol suspiciously until she dug out her volunteer badge.

"Put that thing over your neck," the guard said. "Or you might be mistaken for the inmates and locked in tonight." He chuckled.

"Comedy Central is down at River Center," Carol said.

The guard's chuckle erupted in a full-blown laugh. She did what he said, but shook her head.

At the last minute, Carol turned toward the vet, smiled, and said, "Merry Christmas."

Once inside the dry, warm building, she hurried to her station. Guilt nagged at her. It was her fault those poor people were standing outside in the sleet, waiting to get in. Not only was she ten minutes late, but the only one who bothered to show up to do intake.

The first batch of people streamed in toward Carol's station. The guard would only let in so many at a time. Carol tried to work quickly.

The vet handed Carol his prescriptions. She recognized a couple of the labels from the decades that her baby brother, Eli, battled schizophrenia and depression. She put the bottles in a plastic box and logged them in.

"Any valuables you want in the safe?" she asked.

The vet *gahaphed*. "If I had valuables, you think I'd be staying here?"

"I had to ask," Carol said. "Merry Christmas."

The vet returned the greeting and went to the second station to get bedding, towels, and toiletries.

A sour pungent smell filled Carol's nostrils. She held her breath too late. She could never get used to the stench. But it made her grateful Eli never lived on the streets. Heaviness pushed on her heart. She thought she could help others like Eli by working at SAMM. Instead, it kept the pain fresh, reminding her how her brother battled his demons.

Carol made eye contact and smiled at the woman who stunk. The woman reached her cold hand over the windowless opening and touched Carol's arm.

"No meds. Just wanted to say, 'Happy holidays!'"

At first Carol didn't recognize her. Then she saw the grimy, rawboned man behind her and a name came to her—Jack. No. Jake.

"Merry Christmas to you, too, Iris! How are things going?" Carol wasn't sure how to word that question and not be rude. What were Iris and Jake doing at the shelter? The counselors worked so hard this year to get them jobs at McDonald's on the bus line and an apartment.

"Oh, things didn't work out..." Iris shrugged and launched into her story. It was another employee's fault, then the manager had it out for them. Jake's eyes shifted, his brow furled. The guard scowled at Carol.

"Well, it was nice seeing you," Carol said, interrupting Iris. "Thanks for stopping by."

Jake ambled off toward the second station.

"Next," Carol said.

Iris followed Jake. Sadness settled over Carol. Christmas Eve, of all times, and they had no job, no home—again. She sighed, then plastered on a smile for the next person handing her a brown paper sack of prescriptions.

It was toward the end of Carol's shift when a high-spirited man approached the intake station and shouted, "Doris Day!"

It had been years since anyone had noticed the similarity, but in her younger years men often remarked how much she looked like the famous actress.

The man had no medicine to log in, so Carol said, "Please proceed to the next station."

"Sing '*Que sera, sera*'." He grinned, showing rotted teeth.

The line was backing up. "Go to the next station. Please," Carol insisted.

"Not unless you sing," the man said, not budging.

Carol stood and pointed to the bedding and toiletry station with a stern look.

The man got in the second line. Carol sat and took three prescriptions from the next woman. Before Carol could log the medicine, the boisterous man bolted from the second line and danced in front of Carol again.

"Sing '*Que sera, sera*'," he insisted.

Everything swirled before her—the woman whose medicine needed logged in; the long line of people, wet and cold; and the stubborn man who obviously would not get in the proper line until she did his one request.

"'*Que sera, sera*'," Carol's voice wobbled. She might have been born blonde with a freckled nose like Doris Day, but Carol knew well she was not gifted with the actress's voice. "Whatever will be, will be. Now get back in line!"

The high-spirited man applauded as he started to get in the bedding line. But quickly darted back to Carol's station. "Sing '*Que sera, sera*'."

Carol stood and pointed. "'*Que sera, sera*'. Get back in line!" She sunk to her seat and put her head in hands. The guard glared at her. She finished logging in the woman's medicine as her supervisor slipped into the station.

"Carol," the supervisor said quietly, "It's time to go."

Usually another volunteer came in and relieved her, so Carol felt a bit confused. Still, she gathered her purse and coat and stood to leave.

"Thank you for your service," the supervisor said. "We won't be needing you anymore."

"Wh... why?" Carol asked.

"You couldn't control that man," the supervisor said.

Carol couldn't believe it. She'd been fired! Tears stung her eyes. How could she be expected to control any situation? She couldn't keep the car from hitting her bumper. She couldn't save her schizophrenic brother. No matter what her family did, Eli still died. His heart exploded when he drank a beer after the doctor changed his meds. A drug-drug overdose, they'd called it.

She left the station before anyone could see tears spilling down her cheeks. Carol started toward the door, then stopped.

She wiped her eyes, her face. She couldn't leave. Carol had to pass out cake in the auditorium. Her church held a party for everyone who had a birthday that month. It was a way of celebrating the individuals and ministering God's love to each person.

Sure, she could leave early, and the Youth Group could pass out cake without her. Except last month a man touched her butt when she squeezed past knees to hand someone cake. Carol needed to make sure the girls didn't make the same mistake. The pastors wouldn't know to warn them.

Carol blew air out of her cheeks, took a deep breath, and let it out again. She headed toward the auditorium and birthday party.

Pastor Ingold was leading everyone in singing, "Happy Birthday to you and Jesus." One big red candle burned in the middle of a sheet cake. Hot red wax dripped onto the white frosting. Carol hurried to the Youth Group girls, waiting to serve. Pastor blew out the candle and cut the cake.

Carol directed the teen girls to only pass cake from the aisles. Several giggled when she told them why. The girls handed cake to people at the end of the aisles. But the people farther in wouldn't move, wouldn't help themselves. One of the girls held up the cake plates, as if asking what to do.

Carol huffed. What did they expect her to do? She couldn't make anyone do anything they didn't want to. That was why she got fired. What was the use? Why did she think she could make a difference? She couldn't save Eli. She didn't seem to be impacting anyone's life here either. Look at Iris. No better off than she was a year ago. Why did Carol even bother? She could be at home with her family on Christmas Eve instead.

She started toward the girl nearest her who was about to scoot down an aisle of men despite Carol's warning. Just as she reached out to take the cake from the teen, another black girl came over and offered to help. Only, Carol didn't recognize her from the Youth Group.

"That's okay," Carol said. "We've got it covered." She managed to stop the Youth Group teen and sent her to get more cake and punch.

"Me and my family don't take handouts," the black girl said with an accent Carol couldn't place. "I'll pay our way."

"Where is your family?" Carol asked.

The girl pointed to a tall willowy dark woman in the back row wearing a headscarf and long black cloak-like dress. Three other children, ranging in size like stair-steps, surrounded her. The Youth Group teens brought trays of cakes and punch to Carol. She took one tray.

"Let this young lady help you." Carol nodded her head toward the black girl with the musical accent.

Carol took the goodies to the mother and her children. The children were clean and neatly dressed. Cases like this were usually domestic abuse. How sad, especially at Christmas.

"Would you like some cake and punch?" Carol asked the children and smiled at the mother. The youngest, about three or four, hid her face in the folds of her mother's skirt. The older two seemed eager for the sweets, but asked their mother's permission first. Even Carol's grandchildren weren't that polite.

The mother allowed the children to have the cake and punch. Carol went to hand the mother cake, then gasped.

"Oh!" She looked closer. Nestled inside a sling lay a sleeping infant with wooly black hair. He was as tiny as a doll. "How old?"

"Two days," the mother said.

"Two days!" Carol was taken aback. What was this woman doing at a homeless shelter with a newborn?

As if she could read the shock on Carol's face, the woman said, "My father-in-law died. My husband, he went to South Africa for the funeral. We live in Louisiana. Friends in San Antonio invited us to visit. The baby, he come early. When I come home from the hospital, the people where I stayed were drunk and fighting. It was not safe for my children. We left and had nowhere to go."

Carol felt ashamed for thinking the worst of this woman's husband. "You did the right thing," she said. "You'll be safe here."

Carol put the cake on a chair beside the African mother and held out her arms to hold the baby. Two days old. A Christmas child. God's breath of hope. The infant turned its head toward Carol and mewed like a kitten. She stroked his cheek with hers.

Carol looked up at the teens. Somehow, they'd gotten the people to get up, and do "The Wave" like at a football game, then meet the girls at the end of the aisles to fetch the cake and punch. The administrator had been wrong. It wasn't up to Carol to control anyone. It was her job to help. That was all. To be the hands and feet of Jesus. To be the voice of Good News.

And right now, that was exactly what she was doing. Using her hands to swaddle this precious newborn. Using her feet to rock the infant. And using her voice, wobbly and off-key as it was, to sing a lullaby to this Christmas miracle.

Choose

Vicki Woodson

The land falls into darkness
Another day ahead
Searching for a savior.
Looking in all the wrong places
Not in others.
However good
Not in myself.
However I try,
Only in one
The Way the Truth the Light.
Jesus Christ, who chose to sacrifice
Himself for me, for you, for the world.
Choose this day whom you will serve.
It is your choice,
Light or dark.
Choose life.
Choose Light.
Choose Jesus Christ.

Divine Intervention

Lisa Bell

Seated in a church classroom, I waited for the members of our writing group to arrive. The month before, I challenged each person to write a short nostalgic piece—a memorable moment to share. They didn't disappoint.

As we circled around the room taking turns reading, my sister passed out copies of her document. I smiled. Memories of... me. How could a baby sister not smile at that?

I listened and made notes while she read. Until...

Wait! What?

Did she read what I heard?

I looked down at my copy. My mom had a D&C (dilation and curettage) scheduled when she conceived me? Back then, rabbits died before a doctor confirmed pregnancy. No quick at-home tests in 1960. According to my sister's memory, Mom hadn't even missed a period. She couldn't possibly know I existed—but she did. Somehow.

With four children, the youngest at the time not even two years old, how easily she could have blown off her "gut feeling" and gone ahead with the procedure. No one would have known the doctor cleaning out tissue would have included me, growing in her uterus. But she knew. She sensed my presence—or maybe she remembered a little tryst with Daddy when she failed to use her diaphragm. I mean, they were married after all.

Either way, God's Holy Spirit made sure she knew about a tiny baby no one could see.

I left our group that day tearful, wishing Mom told me that story. In my 50s, I never knew, and wondered how it might have colored my life differently. To know God protected me, literally, from conception still blows my mind.

That truth wasn't my first recognition of divine intervention that spared my life. The first incident happened early in 1985.

I worked at an oil refinery in the billing department. Late one afternoon, my desk phone rang.

My mom, who watched my two daughters while I worked, said, "You need to come home."

No young mother wants to hear those words. "What's wrong? Are the girls okay?"

"Yes. But you need to come home right now." A slight quiver filled her voice. "Leave your car there. Elmer (my then-husband) will pick you up. Wait inside, then go out the back and come home with him."

My mind whirled as I went to tell my boss I had to leave early. What on earth was going on?

Outside, I got into Elmer's pickup, but he didn't know any more than I did. We drove in silence. Thoughts of several situations tumbled through my brain. I couldn't imagine—didn't want to, truth be known.

At my mom's house, I went inside, shocked to see my stepfather there and two strange men. Tall, muscular, confident men. They introduced themselves as DPS officers and showed their badges. My mom took my young daughters out of the room as the officers explained something no one would believe.

"We're here because your ex-husband's brother attempted to hire a hitman to kill you."

WHAT?

Impossible. These things only happen in movies. Right? Not. Everything around me blurred, their words heard but not registering as I tried to make sense of it all.

After years of control and verbal abuse, I broke free from my oldest daughter's father. He subsequently took her out of the United States and kept her for more than a year in a foreign country—one without an extradition reciprocal agreement. I divorced him without his knowledge and gained custody of our baby, even though I didn't have her at the time. Later, he begged me to meet him in Canada, believing if he came back to the United States, they'd arrest him upon entrance. True or not, I got her back and left him behind. I had already remarried and was about four months pregnant with my second daughter when Elmer and I took that trip.

That day, I shuddered as the DPS officers shared their plan.

"We think your ex may be involved, but we've not been able to prove it. And we'll have a much stronger case with a video of the brother paying off our undercover cop."

"Okay." What else could I say to something like that?

One officer continued. "We want to take you to a field by the lake, make it look like the hitman killed you, and take photos. We'll show those to the brother while taping the interaction. Hopefully, when we arrest him, he'll give up your ex."

Elmer jumped in then. "Wait. How do I know you're not the hitman and this is your way to get her alone?"

"You can come with us if you want."

That seemed to satisfy everyone in the room.

The other officer spoke for the first time. "Is there somewhere you can go your ex won't know about?"

"Why?"

"He told the hitman he had contacts—that they'd be watching and would know if he did the job. We don't know who. That's why we came to your mom instead of your husband or stepfather."

That explained the secrecy.

Elmer's sister lived about 30 minutes away. After he called her, we chose that as our overnight getaway. My daughters would go with us.

With the sun waning, we climbed into the back seat of an unmarked vehicle, planning for Elmer to go by our house later to get what we needed. I, on the other hand, would remain hidden until they made an arrest.

During the drive, my brain couldn't process reality. Numb, I rode along without a word, trembling. Not long before we reached the lake area, the officer pulled into a bait and tackle store and came back out with a small paper sack. Weird. What on earth did he need at a time like that?

We drove around the lake looking for a secluded spot. Finally, he stopped. The sun rested just above the horizon. Out in the chilly evening air, the DPS guy pulled a round container from the brown bag.

"Blood bait."

Huh? Apparently, the common fish bait strongly resembled the look of a gunshot to the temple.

I lay in the tall grass, trusting God and these men with my life. They strategically placed a blob of the stinky fish bait on my temple, directed me on how to pose, and placed a newspaper on top of me—to show the date I supposedly died.

"Hold your breath and don't blink." The officer held up a camera.

I took a deep breath. Held it and put on the best blank stare I could. I waited for what seemed forever while the DPS guy took photos. Worst of all, I couldn't move to swat a stupid mosquito that must have had a super long snout on it. The insect pierced all the way through the surface blood bait deep into my temple.

Wow, my first, and only, sting operation. Not anxious to do that again—ever.

Long story short, months later, I testified against my ex-brother-in-law. The jury convicted him and sentenced him to 45 years in prison, but he never implicated my ex-husband. Neither did he serve much of that time, but as a foreigner, INS deported him.

Ironically, on that night when I lay in the field, a tiny baby girl grew in my womb. I didn't know about her yet, but she lived because a man couldn't bear the thought of a child growing up without her mama. The original intended hitman went to a sheriff's deputy he trusted and started this entire event. Had his murderous plot succeeded, my third daughter would have died with me.

Those two events alone should make me feel amazed at how God protected me. But maybe I needed more. Too stubborn sometimes.

On August 18, 2017, I woke with a severe headache. Earlier that week, I experienced tingling in my left arm and hand. After doing online research, I convinced myself it wasn't serious. Couldn't be a stroke—I determined that by having a conversation with myself one night. But that Friday—oh, how my head pounded. At a chamber of commerce lunch, I literally dozed off. Thankful I didn't live far away, I went home, took aspirin and acetaminophen, and fell asleep for several hours. That evening, I went to a potluck concert, but my head throbbed. Again, I dozed off.

Driving home, everything around me looked strange, sort of fuzzy. My heart pounded while my hands shook. What the heck? Nearing my neighborhood, I found myself not at home. Lost, wondering how to get home. I couldn't see well. Living outside the city limits, we had few street lights, which didn't help.

I prayed, "Lord, just get me home where I can be safe."

It never occurred to me I might need emergency care. I finally found my house and got inside, changed into pajamas, and took more painkillers. I slept off and on, but the pain never stopped.

The next morning, August 19, 2017, I woke to the sound of my phone ringing. It always rested on my bookcase headboard, but it didn't seem to be there despite the continued ringing. When I found it, my left hand wouldn't hold it for me to return or make a call. Tears flooded my eyes because of the pain and fear. Something was very wrong. But I couldn't process anything.

Eventually, I crawled out of bed and tripped my way to the bathroom. A hot shower. That'd make my head feel better. After washing my hair, I slumped down in the tub and let the water run over me. I woke up later, the water cooled. How long did I lounge in the tub with water running over me? Somehow, I put on clothes and made it back to the bed.

A thought entered my mind. I should call my daughter. The thought dissipated as quickly as it came, with no clear idea of how to do that.

The guy I was dating at the time came by, but didn't take me to the ER. Fortunately, he had car trouble after leaving, and a policeman pulled him over for driving on the shoulder. The police officer listened to his concerns about me and called EMS.

The paramedics arrived, couldn't get me to answer the front door, and went to the back of my house. I heard someone knocking and opened the back door. Within minutes, they suspected mini-strokes (TIA—transient ischemic attack) with the potential for something more serious.

My second to the youngest daughter and her husband showed up on the back deck where the paramedics checked my vitals. I later learned my boyfriend contacted my sister, who called my daughter because she lived less than ten minutes from me. I had no idea how or why they all showed up at my house.

Assisted by the paramedics, I walked to the end of the deck and down six steps to a waiting gurney. They loaded me into the ambulance and transported me to an airstrip down the road where a helicopter waited to transport me. They planned to fly me to Fort Worth, but with no visible clouds, a storm kicked up between Granbury and that hospital.

Someone said, "We're rerouting you to Providence."

"Okay." I had no clue what that meant, and honestly didn't think about it. They took me to Providence Hospital in Waco, Texas.

The medic asked if I'd ever had morphine, to which I replied, "No." Did they give me some? Maybe. I didn't care if it released my head from the vise holding it in a death grip. Those attending me put headphones on me, which quietened the noise of the helicopter.

I awoke sometime later in a hospital room with my family encircling me. They'd driven to Fort Worth, not knowing about the rerouting, so I'd been out of it for at least a few hours. They told me I suffered a stroke—not merely TIAs. My left hand still didn't function right, and I couldn't see in my left peripheral vision.

So that's why I got lost Friday night? Didn't figure that out until about six weeks later when I went for a walk in my neighborhood.

Several days and multiple pokes, prods, tests, and diagnoses later, they released me. I stayed with my sister for several days. (Yes, the one who wrote the memorable story about my very first days in utero.) Within ten days, my hand worked again. I could see in my peripheral vision. The information processing—well, that took months to reroute the wiring in my brain.

Since that day, I've not had another stroke and no heart issues. That itself is miraculous. No major remnants of a full-blown stroke remain, although at times the information processing slows down a little.

A few months after the stroke, I met with one of the paramedics and the helicopter medic who treated me. I asked how I could tell when the stroke happened.

"The only way we can nail down a time range is to ask someone when that person acted normal and when they didn't."

I shuddered as I processed what he said. I had the numbness in my hand, and then eventually the vision issues. But the slurred words didn't show up until later. The headache should've been a red flag for me and others I saw that Friday. By the time I suspected something serious, I didn't have the cognizance to consider a call to 9-1-1. By Friday night, I was most decidedly not normal. That means at least 17 or 18 hours passed from the time I lost vision until help arrived. Statistically, I probably should have died that day. Most stroke victims have recurring strokes or accompanying heart attacks. Once again, I can point only to divine intervention.

When I think about these three events, I wonder how many times angels guarded me in times of danger. Were there more unknown threats than these three instances when God said, "Not yet."?

For more than 20 years, I knew God had a plan for me beyond mediocrity. I surrendered to it around 2005. I still don't know the full extent of His plans for my life, but I'm not finished yet. Obviously. Why else would God spare my life so many times? Much of what I do every day fits my call of writing and teaching.

Does He have more in mind? It wouldn't surprise me.

This I know… Jesus loves me. The Bible says so, but I know so. He's been with me even when someone, or something, isn't pursuing my life. I feel Him and know He's real—from conception until now and beyond.

*For he will order his angels
to protect you wherever you go.
They will hold you up with their hands
so you won't even hurt your foot on a stone.
(Psalm 91:11-12 NLT)*

Impromptu Lullaby

Mary-margaret Belota

My voice carries barely more substance
than a whisper,
and I move ever more gently
with each approaching step.
You tense for escape, but choose to stay,
the brown of your fur blending seamlessly
against the tan gazebo post where you huddle.

Triple digits came early to Texas this year,
so last night's cooling rain is a welcome respite,
though it will soon rise in steam,
and the sheltering shade
will disappear degree by degree
with the angle of the sun.

You've not let me this close before.
With minimal movement
I ease onto the chaise longue
and switch from murmurs to music,
singing softly
at the low end of my soprano range,
segueing into a wordless version of
"Morning Has Broken,"[1]
and completing the impromptu medley
with the lullaby my mother improvised
to lull us to sleep.

Your ears swivel
as you sway slightly on your haunches,
and your eyes so round,
begin to flag at half-mast.
I resume humming,
and they close completely.

Such gifts God gives:
a quiet back yard
shaded by crape myrtles
and hackberry trees still spring green;
doves cooing;
a brilliant pop of red
in a cardinal sitting atop the fence;
and a mere two feet away,
one small rabbit,
sound asleep. [2]

---

1. Lyrics: Eleanor Farjeon, 1931; Music: Scottish Gaelic tune "Bunessan"

2. Belota, M.-m. (2024). *Johnson County Line" Poems of Texas and the Southwest.* Screened Porch Publishing

Pre-Christmas Pecan Ritual

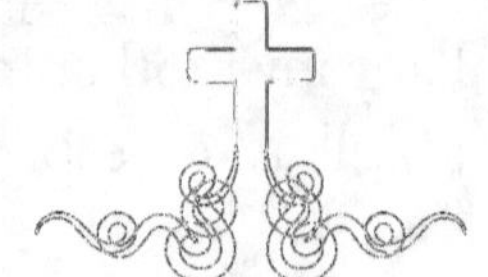

Barbara Boothe Loyd

My maternal grandmother, Mama Jeanne, made fruit cakes every fall like many other Southern women. I recently discovered a small food-dappled recipe in her handwriting for her famous Dark Fruit Cake. The home-grown pecans from her farm in Marksville, Louisiana, enriched her whiskey-sprinkled cakes. They linger on my palette of memories.

As part of her lengthy stays with us in Baton Rouge from 1960 on, she arrived before Thanksgiving laden with paper grocery bags full of fresh, fat, speckled tan and black pecans. On the first Saturday after her arrival, we began our communal ritual of shelling the nuts. My mother, older sister, younger brother, and I joined Mama Jeanne around our Formica and chrome kitchen table. She instructed us to separate the pecans. We set aside any perfect halves so she could use them as her cakes' top decorations. All pecan bits and pieces were placed in other jars so they could be minced for the cakes' rich interiors later.

Mama Jeanne taught me to use the squeeze-type, silver-colored nut crackers which came in a set. The picks were used to remove any remaining nutmeat from cracked shells. Adults with larger, stronger hands cracked the shells first, then the smaller, slender fingers of we younger participants applied the shiny picks to dislodge the lush pecan meat.

At one of our pecan-shelling gatherings, I discovered my allergy to their shells. Ink from newspapers affected me similarly. A runny nose and itchy hands were symptoms. After I announced my discomfort, my mother and older sister peered at me intently when I announced, "I cannot handle these pecans."

After I showed them the rash on my hands, their expressions softened. Since I couldn't work on the pecans, I volunteered to change records on our player to keep the crackers and pickers entertained. I played requests from the work crew and always managed to play the 45 record we had of "Jingle Bell Rock," written by our cousin Jim Boothe from Sweetwater, Texas. It was my favorite Christmas song. My grandmother sang along with us even though her opera-trained voice cracked a little.

When we visited my grandmother at her house in the country, it was pecan harvesting time. We hit the trees' pecan-laden limbs with long bamboo fishing poles to encourage them to drop to the ground. Often, the nuts thumped our heads a few times as they rained down. Most clumps of shells were ready to shed their thick black coverings before they filled our buckets. Even though we wore sweaters, gloves, and jackets while harvesting pecans, the fall chill inspired us to slap our arms to keep warm. Soon, we hopped around and whooped like Indians while the chickens ran to feast on the pecans covering the ground.

Mama Jeanne said, "Any missed pecans will become treats for the chickens."

Their small beaks cracked pecans without much apparent effort. We stomped and hopped on the shells hidden in the grass along with fallen leaves. Our little warm-up efforts helped Mama Jeanne's feathered friends have a feast.

Every autumn, the aisles in Walmart or a grocery store contain stacks of shiny candied fruit as well as the same type of nutcrackers we used. They remind me of the good times shared with my fun grandmother as she assembled and created her fruitcake masterpieces.

Angels (A Revelation)

J. W. Dickson

*"For He will command His angels concerning you, to
protect you in all your ways."*
Psalm 91:11 NAS

God took my weaknesses, fear, and worry, and gave me the strength and stamina to become a mom where grace and mercy followed me and hope and joy led the way. Sometimes, songs helped me endure the changes in life. When you walk through a storm, hold your head up high and don't be afraid of the dark. At the end of the storm, there's a golden light and the sweet silver song of a lark. I never thought my life would be anything but ordinary.

Growing up in a broken home, I was angry, bitter, and lost. Moving away from my childhood home and friends only made things worse. I felt like a failure, constantly seeking approval from parents who were too wrapped up in their struggles to notice mine.

In the college gym where I worked part-time while I went to college, a choir set up on the basketball court, practicing. The moment they started singing, I felt something I couldn't explain. Goosebumps crawled up my arms, and suddenly, I wasn't in that gym anymore. I stood in front of an angelic host glowing with divine light. The vision overwhelmed me. I felt so small—so insignificant. But as quickly as it came, it vanished.

Everything changed the day I heard that choir sing. I shook it off, dismissing it as some kind of stress-induced hallucination. But the vision kept coming back, nagging at me. I tried to ignore it, throwing myself into my work and studies, but the supernatural kept intervening in my life.

Bad choices, struggles, and confusion followed me like a shadow. I felt like I was drowning. No matter how hard I prayed, I couldn't find clarity. Then came the breakup.

Heartbroken and desperate, I cried out to God. "Lord, if you drive the bus, I'll get on."

It was a moment of surrender, and it led me back to my old house, to a concert where Joan Baez sang "Amazing Grace and Scarlet Ribbons," a song from my childhood choir. That night, something shifted inside me. I felt a new strength, a new purpose.

But life wasn't done testing me. I found out I was pregnant, and though I was scared, I chose to keep the baby. My son was born with a heart defect, and the doctors told me he wouldn't survive without surgery.

We moved to Dallas, where the only specialist who could help him was located. I lived with my mom and sister, working at a bakery and trying to make ends meet. The night before his surgery, I carried my son into the house and laid him on the couch.

He looked up at me and said, "Momma, I want to go home."

My heart broke. "You are home, son."

He closed his eyes and said again, "No, Momma. I want to go home."

I hung my head and cried, not knowing if he meant this world or the next. I sang his favorite song to him.

> *"The B I B L E,*
> *That's the book for me;*
> *I stand alone on the Word of God,*
> *the B I B L E."*
> Anonymous, Public Domain

In the hospital room the night before surgery, Sean and I curled up in the bed.

"Momma, we are all alone here."

I hugged him tighter. "No, son, Jesus is here with us."

The surgery went well, but the doctors were baffled. "I don't know how this child has lived a day in his life with a heart like that," one of them said, frustrated.

I knew it was a miracle. I prayed every day for him to live, because I loved him so much. But even with his survival, I struggled. I prayed for him to live, but I also prayed for God to take him home if he had to suffer.

That night, as I lay on the waiting room floor, someone called my name. "Ms., we had to restart his heart."

They took me in to see him, and though his body was still, his hair looked alive, shiny and golden. I touched his head, kissed him one last time, and left the room. In the hallway, I felt goosebumps on my shoulders and heat in my heart. I looked up at my husband and asked if he felt it.

"Felt what?" he said. "No, I didn't feel anything."

That moment left me questioning everything. Was it a sign? A reassurance? I didn't know, but it pushed me to seek answers.

I started reading the Bible, studying it like it was silver and gold. I prayed for the power to stand on the Word of God. But the supernatural didn't stop.

One night, my oldest daughter woke up screaming, clawing at the wall, calling her brother's name. I quieted her, but the experience shook me. Later, I woke up choking, feeling a dark presence holding me down.

I shouted, "Get out, and get back, in the name of Jesus!"

The presence left, and I sat up, grateful for the power of prayer. As I grew in faith, I started sharing my experiences with others. At a grief seminar, I met people who had lost loved ones, and together, we found solace in our shared sorrow. My faith became my food, and I sought wisdom and knowledge like treasure.

One day, I met a man named Kip. He was a sign painter with a thick Irish accent and a story. He had lost his wife and six children in a train accident in Ireland, and afterward, he traveled around in a van painted with scriptures, helping others. Meeting him was a turning point for me. He reminded me that even in the darkest times, we can find light by helping others.

In a church service, a prophet named Ivan Tate, who had the gift of knowledge, ministered to some people in the congregation. He had them stand up, gave them scriptures to confirm what he told them about their lives, and the message God wanted them to have.

He had my brother, Richard, stand up. "Stop living after the flesh. Know ye not that your body is the temple of the Holy Spirit who is in you, whom you have received from God? You are not your own, you were bought with a price. Therefore, honor God with your body." (1Corinthians 6 19-20 KJV).

Then he had me stand up. "You would have died had you not seen the hand of God in the land of the living. He has healed your heart. You will sing and dance for the Lord." Psalm 27:13, 1Samual 16, Psalm 30:11-12, Isaiah 61:3 "To them that mourn in Zion, to give unto them beauty for ashes, the oil of joy for mourning, the garment of praise for the spirit of heaviness, that they might be called trees of righteousness, the planting of the Lord, that He might be glorified." (KJV)

Years passed, and I built a new life. I became a teacher, finding passion and purpose in helping others learn. I remarried my husband, who had found sobriety through AA and then helped others struggling with addiction. We bought a small ranch with twelve acres and three horses—the dream I vowed to fulfill as a child.

But the dream wasn't complete. I knew there was more—a bigger vision of 91 acres, a place of refuge, retreat, and restoration. I didn't know when or how it would happen, but I trusted that in God's perfect timing, it would.

For now, I wait. I sort through keepsakes and heirlooms, preparing for the next season. I cherish meaningful memories with my family and friends, celebrating birthdays and baseball games, knowing each moment is a gift. The celestial conflict that once felt so distant is now a part of my story. I've seen angels and felt the presence of something divine. I've fought darkness with prayer and found light in the most unexpected places. This is my journey, a story of faith, struggle, and redemption. And it's not over yet.

My dad told me years ago, "Climb every mountain until you find your dream."

I am still climbing. I can't just sit down. Life has not been all good, but it has not been all bad. We all need to fight fear with faith, declare the works of God, shine our lights for all to see God's glory, and continue to seek wisdom and knowledge like silver and gold. To pray boldly for our needs and give thanks joyfully for the answers every day.

Angels in Armor

J. W. Dickson

High above the horizon, the angel army's fighting.
In battle gear, the prayers of saints,
Raging warriors of fiery strength.
Fight fierce oh angels in armor,
For the faith of saints and the souls of men
Security, the future and the children.

Hopeful, Thankful and Blessed,
always blessings and peace, JWD

Honoring Mom on Mother's Day

Wanda Strange

*"A Mother is not a person to lean on,
but a person to make leaning unnecessary."*
Dorothy Fisher

"I asked if I could have more than one guest for the Mother's Day Tea," Mother said.

Two of her three daughters lived close enough to attend the special event hosted by the nursing-home staff. She excitedly anticipated the holiday and proudly announced to all her friends, "My girls will be her for Tea."

Mother chose her favorite outfit. The bright multi-color floral blouse with coordinating pink slacks. With the help of the nursing assistants, she carefully styled her hair and applied make-up. Always meticulous about her appearance, she wanted to look especially nice that day.

When my sister and I arrived, she eagerly waited at the table and greeted us with the biggest smile she'd worn in months.

The staff transformed the usual dining room into a festive tearoom atmosphere. Fine china and a beautiful centerpiece decorated each table. Smiling attendants escorted us to our table and served a delicious menu of finger sandwiches and teacakes. A pianist played the residents' favorite tunes, providing added ambiance.

Mom relished the new experience. She enjoyed southern style iced tea but never tasted hot tea or the traditional teatime treats. She absorbed every detail and appreciated the fuss everyone made over not only her but all the residents.

The challenges of the past year faded as we shared a pleasant visit and made a sweet memory.

While her husband lived, the two of them remained isolated in their room and rarely participated in social activities. In the two months since his death, Mother engaged fully in the happenings around the home. Using her career skills as a cosmetologist, she even manicured the fingernails of some of the residents.

Joining her friends at their assigned dinner table, her personality blossomed, and her social circle enlarged. She particularly enjoyed introducing her children and grandchildren to her new friends.

She relished musical entertainment from visiting ensembles and choirs. Several months earlier, a group of friends and I sang at Harbor Lakes, where my mother lived. While we sang gospel standards, many of the ladies and gentlemen sang along.

Later my friend shared, "Wanda, I wish you could have seen your mother's face—she beamed. She was so proud of you."

The encouraging words of my friend touched me and started a healing process. Over the years, I sought to win my mother's approval but never felt assured of her unconditional love.

A shared experience of a simple tea party provided an affirmation of her love and pride. She spoke of each of her children in loving terms and beamed with pride as she boasted of our accomplishments to her friends and to the staff. She introduced us to everyone who stopped to listen as she spoke of all her family.

The afternoon passed quickly with pleasant conversation and ended much sooner than Mother or either of her daughters wanted.

Five months later, Mother slipped away from this world and took her flight to heaven. If we had known this would be our last Mother's Day together, we might have lingered longer.

The priceless memory of a 2011 Mother's Day tea brings a sweet smile to my face. I visualize Mother excitedly experiencing each detail and enjoying her girls. Memories of happy times we share comfort my heart. I look forward to the day we celebrate Mother's Day in Heaven. I anticipate a banquet with the finest of everything, much grander than any tea party we can imagine.

I learned much from my mother.

When I look in the mirror, the reflection resembles her more and more as I age. I hear her words involuntarily escaping my lips—sometimes words of wisdom—others caustic comments of a critical spirit.

Though an imperfect human, like all of us, she exhibited many good qualities. I chose to emulate her generosity, passion for helping others, and her love of music.

In her unique way, Mother encouraged me. She proudly acknowledged her talents and encouraged her children to explore our passions. When I tearfully recounted adolescent stories and feelings of inadequacy, she admonished me, "Always remember, everyone is important. They put their pants on the same way you do—one leg at a time. You are just as good as everyone else. By the same standard, you are no better than anyone else. Treat everyone with the respect they deserve."

I am definitely my mother's daughter. I bristle at injustice and stand up for the disenfranchised. Helping others provides my greatest satisfaction. Confidence in personal skills allow me to appreciate the abilities of others. Respect for individuals and celebration of their unique gifts creates the atmosphere of acceptance. Every person I encounter offers something of value and adds an interesting dimension to my life.

My mother taught me well.

Honoring parents involves much more than obedience and caring for them. By becoming a person of character—the daughter or son a parent celebrates and speaks of with pride—we bring honor to the parents who raised us.

"A mother's daughters (and sons and grandchildren) are her treasures."

Author Unknown

Room for the Holy Spirit

Mary-margaret Belota

Tight spaces scare me. I blame my brother for holding a pillow over my head when we were kids, but truth be told, my struggle with claustrophobia began before the pillow incident.

It influenced my choices for most of my life. No seeing how many people could fit into a phone booth or a Volkswagen Beetle for me!

The activities that interest and engage me do not involve cramped quarters. I write. I sing. I cook. I sew. If crawling under the house or climbing into the attic are necessary, I simply hire (or beg) someone else to do it, which serves me quite well.

When I lived in New York City, crowded subways and buses posed a dilemma, but nothing a little creative maneuvering couldn't solve. Walking twenty-two blocks twice a day at a brisk New York pace eliminated the rush hour transportation predicament, while adding the benefit of enhanced health and well-being.

Elevators, however, practically paralyzed me.

In Texas, where I grew up, when elevator doors open, if five or six people are already on the elevator, there's a good chance the person waiting will give a friendly smile, nod, and say, "I'll catch the next one."

This is a foreign concept to a New Yorker. A New Yorker views a packed-to-the-gills elevator as a challenge and pushes in anyway.

My office on the 21st floor represented a lot of stops, even on an express elevator, and every stop increased the likelihood I'd wind up at the back of a crowded car.

To calm my fears, I did what I always do: I turned to prayer.

"Lord, please don't let too many people get on."

"Lord, please don't let me get pressed against the back wall."

"Oh, dear Lord, please, pleeease, don't let this elevator get stuck!"

The fervor of my prayers failed to produce the desired effect. Rather, they took on a frantic nature, yielding more panic than peace.

Slowly, I changed the focus of my prayers to simply asking God to be with me. Unable to articulate anything else, I relied on the promise in Romans 8:26 (RSV) that when we don't know how to pray, "...the Spirit himself intercedes for us with sighs too deep for words."

I now employ a technique I call "Use the Control Where You Have It." Once I start down the road of all the horrible things that *might* happen, I can't escape the feelings of panic. However, by praying for the control not to think about the what-ifs, I find a balance that allows me to function despite my apprehension.

Now back home in Texas, though I live near a large metropolitan area, there is still an atmosphere of wide-open spaces. Consequently, I am rarely troubled with feelings of confinement.

When cancer struck, however, that all changed.

Surgery was essential to remove a small lump in my right breast, but first the surgeon needed to rule out the presence of cancer elsewhere in my body.

I am truly grateful for modern medical technology, but the term "MRI" struck terror in my heart. My Use the Control technique worked for the span of an elevator ride, but an hour-long procedure requiring me to lie motionless inside a tube? Well, that was quite another matter.

I inquired about an open MRI, but the positioning essential for the imaging of the breasts nullified that option.

I fancied asking if they would anesthetize me. Heck, at that point, a tranquilizer dart sounded pretty good. Unfortunately, no such options were available.

Friends offered various ideas for coping, though all advised keeping my eyes closed the entire time. One even suggested I wear a sleep mask so if I accidentally opened my eyes I couldn't see the apparatus right above my face. Not a particularly comforting admonition.

A nurse told me I could request earphones, but the idea of listening to someone else's musical taste ruled that out. However, I realized a musical solution could work.

I began singing as a small child, in Sunday school, church and school choirs, civic choruses, Community Theatre. As teenagers in the 1960s, my sister and I sang folk music with our brother on guitar. As a result, I know lots of songs by memory.

Convinced of the excellence of the plan to sing my way through the MRI, I set about deciding on my "playlist." That's when it hit me. What songs do I know by heart better than any others? Hymns, of course! Words to hymns spring to my mind in times of hardship or grief or joy probably even more quickly than scriptures.

The day arrived, and as the MRI began, I said a prayer, closed my eyes and started singing inside my head:

"Great is thy faithfulness, oh God my father..."[1]

"Standing on the promises of Christ my King..."[2]

"All to Jesus, I surrender, all to him I freely give..."[3]

---

1. *Great Is Thy Faithfulness,* Words: Thomas A. Chisholm, 1923 (Lamentations 3:22-23), Music: William M. Runyan, 1923

2. *Standing on the Promises,* Words and Music: R. Kelso Carter, 1886 (Ephesians 6:14-17)

3. *I Surrender All,* Words: J. W. Van Deventer, 1896, Music: W. S. Weeden, 1896

"Come thou fount of every blessing, tune my heart to sing thy grace..."[4]

"Blessed assurance, Jesus is mine..."[5]

"'Tis so sweet to trust in Jesus..."[6]

"For his eye is on the sparrow, and I know he watches me."[7]

Before I knew it, the procedure ended and, to my total amazement, fear never once crept into my consciousness. On the contrary, I felt a palpable presence, a spirit of spacious peacefulness throughout the entire process.

In the weeks after my surgery, in preparation for chemotherapy and radiation, I underwent other tests similar to, though not quite as confining as an MRI. In each case, I felt the same peaceful presence.

Reflecting on this phenomenon, I realize not all the tight spots in our lives are physical. How many times, in the throes of decision, do I simply fail to make room for the Spirit's presence?

How often do I immerse myself in the busyness of daily life, attempting to rely solely on my own resources, and thereby restrict access to the very One limited by neither time nor space?

I cannot truthfully say my discomfort with close quarters totally disappeared. However, I found a greater truth in its place. In any and every circumstance, I can find God's loving and sustaining presence as near as the air I breathe and as accessible as a thought turned toward Him.

No matter how confining the situation, no matter how tight the space in which I find myself, whether literally or figuratively, there is *always* room for the Holy Spirit.

---

4. *Come Thou Fount of Every Blessing,* Words: Robert Robinson, 1758 (1 Samuel 7:12), Music: Wyeth's *Repository of Sacred Music Part Second,* 1813

5. *Blessed Assurance,* Words: Fanny J. Crosby, 1873, Music: Phoebe P. Knapp, 1873

6. *'Tis So Sweet to Trust in Jesus,* Words: Louisa M. R. Stead, 1882, Music: William J. Kirkpatrick, 1882

7. *His Eye Is on the Sparrow,* Words: Mrs. C. D. Martin, Music: Charles H. Gabriel

רוּחַ הַקֹּדֶשׁ

The Holy Spirit
Ru•ach (spirit, breath, wind)
Ha•kó•desh (the holy)

In the Quiet of a Pale Blue Sky

J. W. Dickson

For those who would paint emotions into pictures,
sculpt moments with rhythm,
listen to the space between seconds,
the beat between movements and
know the joy not of perfection but of progress.

We who are seekers of what has been,
of lessons learned long ago,
from the wisdom of experience to appreciation
of antiquities, may we continue in
the preservation of purity and peace.

Who but the artists, the musicians, and the scribes
will record the challenges that face us?
Who will reflect the changes we have made?
Let each one remember one compassionate deed,
one honest answer, and courageous sacrifice.

May we all declare the works of the Lord and
make sense of the lives we lead in word and deed.
Whether in poetry or in verse, in lyric or in leadership,
let us drive out the chaos with soul songs
in the quiet of a pale blue sky.

Shine your lights for all to see,
Your good works for the Lord's glory
(Based on Mathew 5:16.)

Perfect Imperfection

Amber Whiteaker

Copyright 2025 Amber Whiteaker

The picture above was the best sandwich loaf I've made to date. I know—it doesn't exactly look like it's supposed to but bear with me. There is a lesson in it all.

I measured the ingredients from memory, but I assure you they were all accurate. To decrease the density, I added flour by feel rather than measurement. Kneading it by hand instead of using my stand mixer was essential for getting the right consistency. When the dough was sticky, I added flour. If it felt too dry, I dipped my fingers in oil. The dough was soft and smooth—the way it's supposed to be—and it rose beautifully.

In fact, Abba expanded it like He often does my challah, and I knew it would be too big for my normal loaf pan. The only larger one I own is a silicone pan with semi-rigid sides. I figured it might expand a little but knew no one would complain about wider sandwiches for our grilled cheese dinner that night. The second rise gave me no problems, so I popped it in my oven and set the timer.

Glorious aromas filled my home as I prepared a new client's contract and finished putting away laundry. A working mother's life is all about multi-tasking. Once the timer beeped, I opened the oven door and discovered those silicone sides failed me! My loaf tipped over in the oven and was absolutely NOT the shape of sandwich bread.

I sighed and set it on the rack to cool, brushing away the tears threatening to spill over. My kids are massive *Tuttle Twins* fans and were ecstatic about grilled *flooger* sandwiches for dinner. They weren't wrong. My loaf mimicked the alien-made blobs from that cartoon. I broke down into simultaneous laughter and tears as Adonai tore down the remnants of that idol of perfection in my life.

It's something He's been working on in me—being a "daughter of excellence" without elevating perfectionism. Yes, we are called to "be perfect, just as your Father in heaven is perfect" (Matthew 5:48 TLV). But that kind of perfection is one of wholeness in our peace and rest—found in obedience and submission to our Creator. As Rabbi Daniel Vargus of Beth Israel JMI Hawaii once said, "Perfection is directly related to being whole in the shalom of the Prince of Peace."

When I sliced this bread for our dinner, it was the softest, most flavorful bread I ever made. Abba reminded me that a soft and flimsy vessel cannot contain real perfection. When we discover our wholeness, our perfection, in the only One who is truly perfect, we *will* overflow our vessel—our potential—our self-imposed boundaries. After tearing down the idol of false perfection, we can experience the authentic version. Adonai's strength is the only thing able to keep us upright. His perfection tastes better than anything we can hope to produce alone. And that grilled cheese was perfect imperfection!

Seeking Contentment and Peace*

Cynthia Tippett

We're going to the ranch! I get to see Henri!

Annie scrunched down in her seat and dreamily gazed out the car window.

Look at those horses. I'm riding the black stallion with the white sword on his muzzle, hanging on to his mane, and clenching my knees to his sides. The wind swirling, my hair flying, my breath hiccupping to the drumming of his hooves. What freedom!

"Annie, sit up! You're slouching." Mom turned around and glared at her daughter. "When we get to Aunt Dot's house, I want you to act nice and greet everyone. Don't run off with your cousin and disappear to who-knows-where."

The horse stumbled, and Annie went over his head like a bullet. The ride was over, and the daydream ended. Annie sat up and brought her hands together, pushing them into her stomach. She grimaced and bit her bottom lip.

"Daphne, your leg is on my side. Move it!" Annie kicked Daphne, and the intruding leg moved to its rightful place. Annie smiled. Her younger sister stuck out her tongue in reply. Annie kicked her again.

"Mom!" Daphne complained. "Annie kicked me."

"Annie, quit bothering your little sister, and act like you're fifteen instead of three. We're nearly there. Straighten up."

Mom always blames me for everything. Daphne's the little sweetheart.

Annie pinched herself on the right arm.

I need a cigarette. Hurry up, Dad, and get us there!

Annie again gazed out the window, sitting up straight this time. She thought back to the Saturday a week earlier...

"OK, y'all. Be quiet and put your foot only where I step. Some of them creak." Annie slowly placed her right foot at the right edge of the stair. "See?" she whispered.

The three teenagers behind her followed her lead, and the four silently and carefully crept down the stairs. "Now crawl in front of the door so you won't break the moonlight," Annie told the girl behind her. "Pass it on."

All four dropped to their knees and followed Annie, giggling quietly.

"Shhh! My parents' bedroom is right over there." Annie pointed to her left and continued crawling through to the library. She stood, and the girls following her did the same. Annie grabbed the three into a huddle. "We're now going out the kitchen door, but still walk softly, and keep quiet!"

Constance, Amelia, and Emma are quiet now. I can hear their shallow breaths. Are they as excited as I am? Will we get away with it? This is my first time to sneak out. I've planned it well. Just out through the kitchen door and home free.

Annie patted her pocket.

I've got cigarettes and a lighter. Just have someone get us some beer—probably Billy. He'll be making the drag, and we'll flag him down. Get a ride from him to the county line for beer.

The grandfather clock in the hallway struck the first chime of eleven o'clock, and Annie jumped. The other three gasped, and all four stopped.

"Hhhh," Annie sighed.

She waved them onward. They crept through the kitchen, into the utility room, and then the door. "OK. Unlock and open, and out we go."

Cool, moist air met their open mouths. The four snuggled into their coats, went down the steps, and onto the driveway.

CRUNCH. CRUNCH.

The gravel complained beneath their shoes as the girls scurried to the street.

"Billy will be by shortly. He said he'd watch for us. Are y'all OK?" Annie met the three pairs of eyes. Three heads nodded. "Let's start walking to the drive-in. He'll see us and stop."

The girls walked west.

Annie watched the headlights coming toward them. "There's Sally. Move on, Sally," she yelled as the car slowed down. Soon the headlights of a 1967 Dodge Charger came toward them.

"That's him!" She waved.

SQUEALLLLL...

The Charger came to a stop. Billy rolled down his window. "Y'all need a ride?"

"Billy! Just the guy we want to see. It's cold. Got the heater going?" Emma ran to him. She kissed him and jumped in the front passenger seat. Constance, Annie, and Amelia crawled into the backseat and hugged each other to create some warmth.

Emma smiled at her boyfriend. She leaned over to kiss Billy again. "Let's go get some beer!"

Annie sniffled. That blond hair always needed brushing, but that face? So handsome. Emma was one lucky girl.

Billy shrugged. "OK, ladies. But since I'm the only one old enough to drink, I'm going to park behind the store, and y'all keep down. Just in case the ABC is there. And stay down until we're back up on the highway. Got it?"

He glanced in his rearview mirror and grinned when three heads nodded in agreement.

Emma pouted. "Billy, we've done this enough times. You don't have to tell us."

"And we haven't ever gotten caught, have we? I just want to keep it that way."

Constance leaned up to the front seat, crossing her hands in front of her. "I want some wine. Can I get some Boones Farm?"

Billy looked in the rearview mirror again. "Yep, if that's what you want. It's awful stuff, though. Sure you don't want something else?" He puckered up his lips. "It's way too sweet for me."

"Yeah, that's what I want. I like the sweetness. And it goes to my head fast, too." Constance flopped back on the seat.

Amelia punched Constance. "That's the real reason you want to drink it. Fast high. Speaking of that, Billy. Got any weed? That's my preferred high."

Billy shook his head. "Nah. But there's a party at Neal's. We'll go after we get our booze. You can probably find some there."

Amelia smiled back at him in the rearview mirror. "Yeah, party!"

"Are we at Neal's place already?" Amelia looked out the window. Teenagers and young adults stood around a fire. They scattered as Billy maneuvered the car around them.

"My gosh, girls. My car stinks. Didn't you crack your window when you smoked?" Billy rolled down his window and stopped the car.

Cold, fresh air replaced the sweet, bready beer smells and rancid cigarette smoke. A blast of Three Dog Night's "Mama Told Me" bombarded the car, and laughter and the smell of acrid pot wafted in through the open window.

"We're at Neal's party. Get your butts moving." Billy cajoled the seemingly inebriated girls from the backseat. He opened his door, went around the car, and opened both passenger doors, helping Emma from the front seat.

"Emma, we're going to have to help these younger girls to the house. They're way too drunk to walk by themselves. You can help Annie, and I'll walk with Amelia and Constance."

"Thansh you, Emmmmma," Annie slurred as Emma pulled her up from the backseat.

"Where are we? I can walk by myselsh." Annie yanked her arm away from Emma and fell from the car. She giggled as she lay sprawled on the ground. "I guesh not."

Emma stood over Annie. "I'm gonna get you up. Hang on to me this time, Annie Jane, and don't let go!"

The five stumbled to the door of the house, which Billy opened while Constance and Amelia leaned on him for support. Neal sauntered over and took Amelia's hand.

"Come with me. We'll stay outside and take a few tokes of weed before we go in. That good with you, Amelia?"

"Yes. I'm Ok. I just drank three beers since leaving the liquor store at the line, and I'm wanting to smoke some grass. Lead on, my white knight."

Billy rescued Emma from Annie, and he stumbled when Annie nearly fell again.

"Emma, we shouldn't have let her drink so many beers. How many did she have? It's only been about an hour since we bought it." Billy looked at his watch. "It's 1:17 a.m."

"I don't know. The case is still in the car. Take Annie over to the sofa and then go out and bring in what's left. Amelia said she had three beers. How many beers did you have, Constance?"

"I had half the Boones Farm. Annie was guzzling the beers quickly and throwing the cans outside. I think she rolled down the window at least five times, maybe more. She's out of it. Don't let her drink anymore." Constance grabbed her head. "I don't think I'm going to drink much more of the wine. I guess we're light weights. But you're seventeen, and Billy's twenty-one, right? So you have a few more years of drinking than us."

Billy walked Annie to the sofa, and she plopped down, giggling. Billy strolled to the other side of the room, took Emma's hand, and kissed her.

"Who are you?" Annie mumbled, as an older man sat beside her.

"I'm Murphy. Don't you remember, Annie?" he said as he placed his arm around her.

"I need to pee." Annie complained and struggled up from the sofa. She staggered to the first door she saw, opened it, and cackled. "It's the closhet." She weaved from side to side and tumbled to the floor. Murphy walked over and pulled her up.

"Let me show you where it is." He led her to the next door on the right and opened it.

"Thish isna the bashroom."

Murphy pushed her on the bed and yanked off her jeans. He fell on top of her.

Annie struggled as a rush of energy entered her body. "No!" she cried. "Get off me!"

Murphy pushed his hand over her mouth.

She bit his palm. Blood oozed over her face.

He cried out an obscenity and threw his arm in the air.

Annie brought her knee up, catching him in the groin.

He rolled to the side of the bed.

Annie jumped up.

"Hmph! You b....!" Murphy yelled.

The door opened, and Emma and Billy rushed in.

"He, he, he...." Annie gasped while pulling up her jeans.

"You don't need to say. I can see." Emma frowned and hugged Annie.

"I'm glad you're here," Annie shakily mumbled, her face in Emma's shoulder.

Emma hugged her harder. "Let's get you cleaned up. Billy, find Amelia and Constance. We're outta here."

Billy grabbed Murphy and slammed him down to the wood floor. "Don't move." he commanded. "You stay there, and don't say a word."

Murphy wiped his bloody hand on his jeans and glared back at Billy. "I..."

"Not a word!" Billy repeated and stomped out the room.

Emma walked out of the house, her arm around Annie. Billy beckoned Constance and Amelia. The five of them scrambled into the car. Billy turned on the ignition, and they spun out toward town.

Constance asked, "Why did we leave in such a hurry? It's just a little after 2, and I thought we would stay at least until 3."

Emma looked back at the three girls. "Billy and I wanted to leave. We need to get you girls back to Annie's house."

Constance grabbed Annie's hand. "Have you been crying? What's wrong?"

Emma paused for a minute. "How about you and Amelia come over to my house and stay the night? That way only Annie will have to sneak back in. My mom won't care if you're staying there. You can call your parents after we get up, and I'll take you home. How about that?"

"Is that OK with you, Annie?" Constance squeezed Annie's hand. "We can get our stuff later. How about you, Amelia?"

Amelia was concerned. "Well, Annie, I want to know if you've been crying. You never told Constance if anything's wrong."

"Nothing's wrong," Emma quickly responded. "You're just tired. Right, Annie?"

Annie nodded. "I'd like to be alone."

Sunlight hit her eyes like a flash of lightning. Annie pulled the blanket over her head and groaned.

What woke her?

KNOCK. KNOCK.

Annie groaned again. "Who is it?"

"It's your dad. I need to talk with you."

Annie wearily glanced at the clock. 9 a.m. Her head throbbed.

What can Dad want? I didn't get to sleep until around 6 this morning, but I'll get it over with, whatever IT is.

"Ok. Come in."

The door opened, and her dad loomed in its entryway. "Annie, I have something to discuss with you. Are you awake?"

Annie peeked from under the blanket. "Barely."

"I'm sorry I woke you, but this is important. Will you sit up? You need to listen." He sat on the bed.

Annie pulled on her robe from the floor and sat up. "I'm listening."

"I got a call this morning. It was a private detective I hired to follow someone. I'm representing a young woman in a divorce case."

"Yeah?"

"The private eye told me the person he's following said he was with you early this morning, and you gave him a neck full of Hickie's. Is that true?"

"I didn't give anyone a neck full of Hickie's. Who is this guy?"

"I can't say, but were you with anyone early this morning?"

"Whoever he is he's lying!"

"You didn't answer my question. Were you with anyone early this morning?"

"I was here in bed early this morning."

"Annie, where are the girls who were spending the night?"

"Uh...they left with Emma earlier."

"How early? I was up at 7, and I didn't see them leave."

"Oh, sooner than that. Must have been around 6." Annie scooted off the bed and stood.

"So why did they leave with Emma at 6 this morning?"

Annie walked to the door. "I don't know. Emma called and wanted them to come have breakfast with her, so she came and picked them up." She walked toward the doorway. "I've gotta go to the bathroom."

"Where did they go? I don't know of any place in town that opens that early."

"I don't know, Dad. Maybe they went to Emma's house first."

"Something isn't right. You're not telling me the truth."

"Dad, I'm telling you the truth. Call Emma and talk to her. She'll back me up. I'm going to the bathroom." Annie ran out the door.

The bathroom door slammed shut. Annie's father stood up from the bed, and, in long strides, went to the restroom door, knocking loudly. "Annie, your mom, Daphne, and I are going to church in about 45 minutes. I expect you to come with us! See you downstairs."

CREAK, STOMP, CREAK, STOMP.

"Hhhh," Annie signed. She picked up the hall phone and dialed. Three rings. "Hello, Emma? My dad's going to call you, and..."

This pew is so hard.

Annie counted the slats in the ceiling of the church.

The preacher is boring. What is he saying? Mark 1:8. Something about Jesus baptizing with the Holy Spirit. Ha! Where was Jesus when Murphy was on top of me? God, Jesus, the Holy Spirit. And I should repent for my sins? It's all rubbish.

Emma approached Annie in the hallway at school. "Annie, you need to cheer up. Have you told the other girls about what happened?"

"No. I don't think I will."

"Do your parents know? Have you talked to God about it?"

"God wasn't there for me, and I don't think he's around to listen."

"Annie! God is everywhere and will always be there for you."

Annie left her friend, opened the glass door, and walked outside. A tree was to her left with a seat underneath. She slumped to the bench and carefully looked around.

Good. Noone's around.

She lit a cigarette.

I'm going to burn myself. Maybe that will make me feel better. Awww. I like my skin hot and scalding. It doesn't hurt as badly as I feel inside.

She leaned back—a false contentment. A false peace.

The car's slowing down.

Annie glanced out the window.

We're here. I can't wait to tell my cousin about that horrid Saturday. I know she'll commiserate with me.

The vehicle stopped. Annie opened her door and climbed out of the car.

"Henrietta," she called. "Hey, Henri. I'm here!"

Her tall, blonde-hair, blue-eye cousin ran out of the house. The girls hugged.

"So happy you've come. What do you have to tell me? I got your letter yesterday, and I'm anxious to hear."

"Let's go out back, and I'll tell you, but first I need to hug Aunt Dot and Uncle Ted. I have orders from Mom." Annie rolled her eyes.

"Ok. I'll meet you on the porch swing."

"Hi, Aunt Dot." Annie hugged her. "Uncle Ted." She hugged him. "I'm so glad to be here. How are you? Well, gotta go."

She ran to the backyard, jumped on the swing, and hugged her cousin. "How about we walk to our favorite tree, and I'll tell you?"

The two girls, arms around each other, slowly strolled to the big oak tree and stood under its canopy of branches. Annie, crying softly and shaking, relived the past Saturday—the beer, the party, Murphy, everything. And the lies she told her dad Sunday. About going to church. About her hurt, self-loathing. "And God abandoned me."

Henri backed up in shock. "God did not abandon you!"

"OK. God didn't abandon me, because God does not exist." Annie yelled in reply.

An eye-blinding light and a force so strong it threw Annie to the ground suddenly emanated. The raw, verdant earth assailed her senses. Tears streamed from closed, stinging eyes. Ears rang from a booming voice only she could hear.

I AM! I AM THE LORD!

Lord, I didn't mean that. You are my shield. I see now you gave me the strength to fight. You led Emma and Billy to me. How could I say you aren't here? You are everywhere, in the ground I lie on, in my cousin, in me! Will you forgive me?

FORGIVE YOU? WHY?

You know, Lord.

TELL ME.

Please forgive me for drinking beer until I'm drawn away from you. For blaming you when I am the one who lost control. For yielding to the world. For lying to my dad.

AND?

And... and for kicking my sister when I felt bad. And for physically punishing myself in self-loathing. And for not going to you, Lord, when I needed you. Abba, Father. I am not worthy to ask this of you.

YOU ARE WORTHY. I LOVE YOU!

Oh, Lord, do you? You love me? You are everything. I give myself to you.

Annie let the Holy Spirit overcome her.

I am contented. I am at peace.

A tug on her right arm startled Annie.

Was I asleep? Was it a dream? Lord, did you really speak to me?

"Annie! Annie! Are you okay? Say something!"

"Uh, something."

"Smart aleck. I guess you're alright." Henri sighed. "I thought you were hurt awful. What happened? You tumbled to the ground and were mumbling, but I couldn't understand you."

Annie slowly climbed to her feet. "God spoke to me. He said he forgave me, and I was worthy. He said he loved me." Tears dropped from her eyes, which were wide with wonder. "He said that to me after I denied Him. He was always there with me. What a fool I've been."

Grabbing Annie's hand and pulling her, Henri fiercely hugged her cousin. "Don't be so hard on yourself. You're no fool. You're just human. Jesus is the only perfect human. The rest of us are imperfect sinners who need forgiveness. From God. And yourself. You need to forgive yourself also. Do you want to pray?"

Annie nodded. "Let me start. Blessed Father, thank you for kicking me in the knees and bringing me down to worship You. I really needed that. And thank you for loving me when I'm not lovable. You're awesome, Lord. You were always with me, and You saw me when I was lying and hurting myself and hurting others. And still, You love me and say I'm worthy."

Henri continued Annie's prayer. "Precious Lord, we are Your children and need Your Word. Let us not forget Your Word, and give us understanding to bless me and Annie every hour in every day. Through Christ our Savior, we petition this prayer."

And both said, "Amen."

"Let your conduct be without covetousness; be content with such things as you have. For He Himself has said, 'I will never leave you nor forsake you.'"
Hebrews 13:5 NKJV

"Each time he said, 'My grace is all you need. My power works best in weakness.' So now I am glad to boast about my weaknesses, so that the power of Christ can work through me."
2 Corinthians 12:9 NLT

My Momma's Hands

Sarah Olson

HANDS...
tell a beautiful story.
ignite passion,
illuminate paths,
integrate ideas,
seal deals,
heal,
teach,
guide,
hold space for unspoken needs and expectations,
hold space for tears that fall inexplicably
pull strength from the depths of unspeakable places
bring peace in unprecedented times,
create a tapestry weaving lives as fingers intertwine.

There's a depth to grief that is untouchable. Each day warrants a new opportunity to dive into the abyss. (Can anyone who has ever swam in the sea of grief think of a better term than that?) Or dance to the movement of memories.

Today (and most days), I choose to dance to the movement of memories. The principal dancer in this movement of memories? My momma's hands. It's been seven years since my sweet momma left her earthly body. Each day, however, I'm reminded of something very special she left me. Her hands—both physically, and metaphorically.

When I look at my hands, I see my momma's hands. My father and I have talked about it more than once—how Momma left me her hands. The beauty in this noticing is the deeper levels this special piece of her unlocks.

My momma's hands healed. She worked in the medical field diagnosing people's pain. Every day, she selflessly served. Every day, she had the chance to make a difference, a positive impact in this world.

My momma's hands guided. She was a shining example of motherhood from which I am able to draw strength. On the super hard days when my nose is to the grind, and the sound of that last scream from a child puts my body on edge, I look down at my hands. I clinch my fists, take a deep breath, dig my heels in, and draw strength from deep within to keep going. That strength keeps me loving my babies, speaking kindly, compassionately, and from a place of understanding and tender touch instead of reacting in impulsive anger. Momma's hands taught me that.

Momma's hands were passionate. My momma painted and sketched, wrote poems, love letters, and encouraging notes. Art and the written word move me deeply. My momma's hands taught me that.

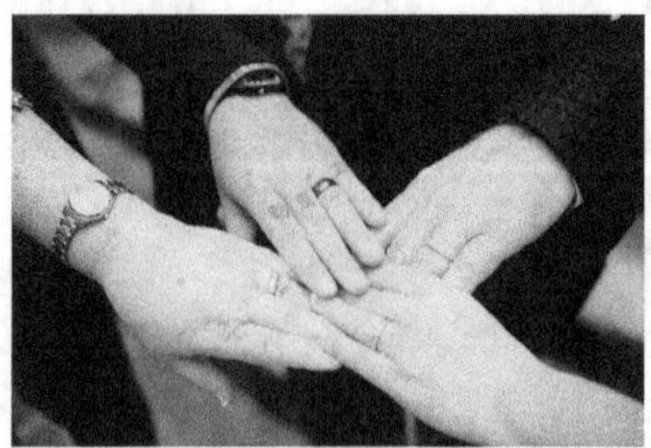

This picture was taken on my wedding day. I asked the photographer to capture my immediate family's wedding band hands. Boy, does it tell a story!

My brother's hand tattoo reads HARD. His (unpictured) right-hand tattoo reads LOVE. Put them together and they say LOVE HARD. His hands tell a story. A story of pain, healing, redemption, love, passion, music, art, and joy.

My daddy's hand holds the stories of so many families. His own, but also those he has ministered to for over 40 years. The countless times he has joined hands not only with his family, but others, as he passionately poured prayers from the depths of his soul into the depths of theirs.

My hands, specifically in this moment, held such a deep respect and honor for the people closest to me represented in this picture, but also a hope for my future, plans for family to pour into, a narrative to develop that has unfolded over the last ten years.

My momma's hands... if they could talk... tell the stories of her legacy being left now as I type these words. I love having my momma's hands.

The Silver Cord is Shattered

Christine Kohler

Miraculous first breath from God, sever the cord
to begin life's journey into veiled mystery
from seed to flesh and bones. Water to earth. We change
body, soul, spirit, our triune being is mortal.
Life struggling into never-ending circles.
Striving forward, a treasured prize of victory.

Scaling Everest-sized mountaintops to victory
depends upon trust and faith in a sturdy cord.
Looping from waist to higher points, in a circle
of mist, veiling the peak from sky in mystery.
Dizzily realizing I am earthbound mortal,
one slip from solid rock and everything will change.

Plunging into unfathomable depths of change
beneath the seas, a SCUBA diver's victory
over breathing, like fish gills, possessing mortal
threads of air from a tank, regulator, and cord.

Making me one with sea creatures, a mystery
deep in time warps before life lands in a circle.

Dipping and yawing, the plane turns in a circle.
Finding a favorable spot, I shift and change.
Ready. Set. Jump! Gravity unravels mystery
free-falling to ground, letting go, taste victory.
Until I have no choice but to pull the rip cord.
A parachute safely lands this earthbound mortal.

Miraculous last breath to God, leaving mortal
body behind. Dust to ashes. In a circle
New Life sprouts again by a shattered silver cord.
We shall not all sleep, but we shall all go through change
Death is swallowed up in glorious victory.
Behold, He shows an inscrutable mystery.

How the Spirit returns to God is a mystery.
For this mortal being takes on an Immortal
body with its soul. Death's sting denied victory.
Incomprehensible, a completed circle.
Without the tethers to Earth, no need for change.
Beyond, unfathomable freedom from a cord.

O, what mystery is an incorporeal cord.
Eternally immortals remain without change.
Abiding victory in Trinity circles.

Imagination

Vicki Woodson

Our assignment for the day involved writing a short story. Sounds easy enough, but not for me. My friend sat behind my desk, picking on me when the teacher looked away. We'd been friends and neighbors since third grade. Despite sharing an eleventh-grade English class, he surpassed me by at least a year.

When my dad suffered a heart attack, his parents looked after me and my sister, allowing my mother to stay at the hospital. I believed I was smarter than he and his older sibling, because I helped them with their homework. Now that I am older, I realize they let me do it, so they didn't have to.

With this mindset, I expected to write a better story than he would. Did I? The short answer is no.

I got an A for correct grammar and he earned a C. My story felt stiff and lifeless, a stark contrast to the exhilaration I imagined his words evoked in the reader. His tale of descriptive imagery took you on a trip, roaring down the road with him on his motorcycle. That day, I determined I possessed no imagination.

Years passed, and although writing a book was a consideration, I could not complete even a simple story. I continued to read various books, with a focus on mysteries. Eventually, I shifted my attention from writing to encouraging my grandson, who enjoyed telling imaginative stories. My role transitioned to supporting others rather than pursuing personal writing goals.

My usual church suspended services for a period during COVID, and after it resumed, I stayed away to protect my elderly clients. Upon returning, I visited the Heights Church and decided it was where God wanted me to be.

One night, they had a service to introduce group leaders, and afterward, to meet them. The writing group captivated me.

This marked my initial encounter with Lisa Bell, the exceptional leader of our writing group. I introduced myself to her and explained my writing interest. I told her I didn't have any imagination but wanted to gain knowledge of the art of storytelling. She took my email to give me the time and address for the meeting. If we were supposed to bring any writing to the group, I might have nothing, but I would be there.

With pens and a notebook by my bed, I prepared for my first group gathering. Was I eager or scared? Maybe it's a stupid idea, but I won't know if I don't try. So, I embraced the challenge.

Uncertain over what to expect, I intended to move forward and find out. Was this God's plan for me? I went to sleep with this on my mind. During the night, I woke from a vivid dream. I sat up in bed, fumbled for the lamp, and grabbed my writing tools. I rubbed my eyes, brushing the sleep away, and I wrote everything I could remember. The words, raw and unpolished, leaped onto the page as I penned them. I reread them, a nervous flutter in my chest. Had I done justice to it? God gave me this dream and the start of my story.

One of my favorite biblical teachers is Andrew Wommack. In his weekly program, he taught on how God gave all of us an imagination. I know! Not a coincidence. My Heavenly Father moved me forward on my new adventure. My initial chapter and the understanding I possessed the ability to be creative. Wow! The Lord is so good to me, and I hadn't even made it to my first appointment.

At the first meeting, I brought Lisa's book, The Sword, and A Pen: 12 Lessons for Christian Writers, along with my pens and tablet. Having written my first chapter, I was ready to start my adventure. After prayer, the three of us in the group got to know one another. Not able to contain my excitement, I blurted I had something to read.

They stared at me, dumbfounded. I told them I lacked imagination and wouldn't have material to read, but there I was. With hesitation, I opened my notebook and read the dream I had penned in the middle of the night. The narrative was about a daughter going to an appointment for her mother's antique business. The fire and the rescue of two small boys provided an exciting beginning for my book.

I looked forward to the group meeting. Every session enhanced my eagerness to further develop my writing skills. Consumed with thoughts of my book and characters, it became a driving point in my everyday existence. The once ordinary life I lived brimmed with excitement and possibility.

This proved to be the chief point of my week. My mind downloaded chapter ideas like one downloads computer files while I worked. Ideas for characters fleshed out. I seized every opportunity to jot them down. My notebook overflowed with plots, character sketches, and even ideas for a second book. Every page reflected the unlocked creativity God gave me.

While I give my Lord all the glory for my new journey, I couldn't have done it without Lisa and DeeDee. They gave me much more than a critique and encouragement of my work—a newfound friendship based on our mutual love of God and writing.

Each week, we went over a chapter of our lessons on writing out of Lisa's book. I learned about Show Don't Tell, Point of View, passive verbs and so much more. Afterward, we read the chapters we wrote to receive help and constructive criticism. My unfamiliarity with the rules of writing hindered my efforts. I was impatient. The week was too long between meetings. Hungry to learn more about the craft, I sought other teachers on the internet. One I found especially helpful was Jerry Jenkins. I soaked in the information. I also listened to Lisa and DeeDee read their contributions. Each time provided valuable insights. Lisa made corrections on my story and always wrote a brief note of encouragement. I couldn't wait to read what she had written. These little snippets gave me the incentive to continue.

Each meeting and group fellowship fostered a sense of belonging and purpose. My ordinary life now held untold potential, revealing a path I had long ignored and neglected. My lack of knowledge held me back, not only in God's Word but not following the road He set before me.

I continued to write, fueled by the encouragement and constructive feedback from my peers. My stories evolved, taking on richer layers and deeper meanings. I transformed from a person who believed she lacked creativity into a dedicated writer, embracing my vision.

Writing transformed both my stories and my personal growth. It became a process of self-discovery, a testament to the power of imagination and faith. And with each word I penned, I grew closer to the calling that brought me to this place.

The beginning of my novel became the foundation of a broader story I was to share. Looking at my fellow writers, I felt certain I belonged there. After receiving inspiration for my novel, I have completed thirty-five chapters of my first draft, two short stories, and a poem. I felt a deeper connection to my faith and calling with each chapter I wrote. The act of writing was life-changing in my walk with God as I relied upon Him to help me pen the words.

Imagination became my guiding light, revealing endless possibilities. I embraced it, knowing that this was only the start of a remarkable journey.

Adopted Twice

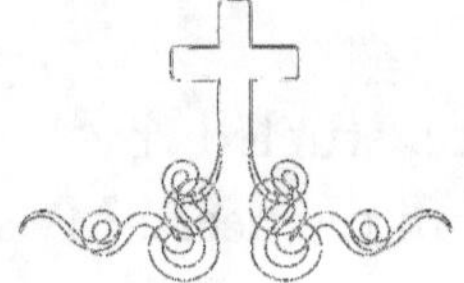

Tony Hatch

"Yes, sir. I did." Those four words softly but courageously uttered by my 11-year-old foster brother, Bobby Shelton, reversed my 10-year-old juvenile delinquent life in an instant.

This was in response to Mr. Shelton's question. "Did you have anything to do with the rock throwing that almost killed the boy next door?"

Mr. Shelton, Bobby's dad and my foster father, had already warned that whoever had any part in throwing rocks at the neighbor would get a hard licking with his belt. He swatted his hand hard for emphasis.

I was the guilty one who threw the rock that hit the kid in the temple and almost killed him. In my mind, I screamed, "Lie, Bobby. Lie!"

Bobby bravely accepted his punishment, gritted his teeth, grimaced, but held his tears back.

Mr. Shelton asked me the same question, and I tried to lie, but the words would not come. I was surprised to hear myself say, "Yes, sir, I did," which resulted in a licking every bit as harsh as Bobby's. My foster brother was the bravest person I knew and became my idol that day.

He also taught me another lesson that has become a part of me. I always thought I was perfect. If anything ever went wrong, I saw it as someone else's fault. One day, kicking a football back and forth, his kick went way off to the side.

He said, "Oh, I'm sorry. That was my fault."

I'd never heard anyone admit fault before. That made it easier when I kicked my ball wild to say, "Oh, I'm sorry. That was my fault." It became easier to admit I'm not perfect.

But it really hurt my feelings when I realized I'm a bit of a weirdo. It had been hard to admit I wasn't perfect, but then I had to accept I'm not even normal. When I found out normal just means average, common, ordinary, I didn't know if I even wanted to be normal. I think I'll just keep being a perfect imbecile.

Following Bobby's example, I went to the extreme and became brutally honest. Surely, God wants us to tell the truth no matter who or how bad it hurts, I believed. Eventually, I came to believe a little white lie can sometimes be merciful, and I hope God forgives me.

I had been a willful, lying, cheating public menace with no desire whatsoever to behave or be rehabilitated. What I wanted was my only compass, and the sooner the better.

My mother was a single mom with my three younger siblings to raise on her own. My dad had an accident as a child.

His doctor apologized to my dad's mother. "He will never be able to father children."

My birth implied that Mom was unfaithful to my dad.

A couple of years later, my Uncle Abe, watching me walk across a field, said to Aunt Clara, "There's not a doubt in my mind whose kid that is. He waddles just like a sailor, just like Gene Hatch."

I have also seen mannerisms, traits, gestures in my son, Tim, that I've seen my dad do or make. I can almost see my dad in my son. There's not a doubt in my mind either about whose kid I am.

Dad was something of a mama's boy and readily agreed to divorce my mother and move back to New York. My paternal grandmother never accepted me.

Mom married again to a Mr. Rollins and gave birth to my brothers, Wayne and Craig, with my sister, Ramona, sandwiched between the two boys. I do not consider them half-brothers and half-sister at all. I thought he was my dad, too, and loved him as such.

Mr. Rollins went into the Army after Pearl Harbor was attacked and was bayoneted in Europe and hospitalized. My mother told me he sent her a letter saying he was going to kill her when he got back home to Mountain View. She seemed genuinely terrified. I don't know the reason for his rage.

I was downtown when I saw him walk into town from the nearest bus drop-off on the main highway about five or six miles from town.

Terrified, I ran right up to him and asked him point blank, "Are you gonna kill my momma?"

He calmly answered, "No."

I ran all the way home, about four city blocks, yelling, "He's not gonna kill you Momma. He's not gonna kill you!"

When he got there, everything seemed normal to me—typical hugs and kisses. I was very relieved and happy.

A few weeks later, Mom said she was going to drive up to the 'Res,' the Wind River Shoshone Indian Reservation, to visit relatives in Lander, Wyoming. Mr. Rollins advised her she needed her brakes adjusted before driving those horrible winding narrow mountain roads. The next day he crawled under the car and had me step on the brake pedal several times while he adjusted the brakes. It took a good hour.

Momma helped Grandma and her friend into the backseat, then had me get in the front passenger seat, and off we went.

We drove along some scary, winding, one-lane dirt roads—some so steep I was terrified we were going to tip over backward and roll back down the hill. But Momma was a good driver. I'd seen her driving trucks like a pro. She looked so pretty hopping down out of the driver's seat of a truck in her English riding britches and high-top, lace-up brown boots. I was so proud of her.

We had just turned a corner and started down a very steep hill. The car picked up speed. Momma pumped the brakes. Then she stomped on the pedal uselessly. My gut tightened as we bounced off the road.

A blur of green and brown rotated counterclockwise as we bounced and rolled sideways several times about fifty yards down the slope—almost into the creek below. We sat there stunned and dizzy for a minute or two before we got the doors open to get out.

Momma and I finally managed to get out, but Grandma and her friend in the back seat couldn't move. We trudged back up the steep incline to the road again, just in time to flag down a big logging truck. The driver took us to get help.

Grandma died of her injuries a few weeks later. I don't know whether her friend died or not. It took me years to put two and two together and accept my conclusion. I firmly believed Mr. Rollins messed the brakes up to kill my mother. He killed Grandma instead.

The facts:

1. Mr. Rollins told my mother he was going to kill her.

2. He advised her she needed the brakes adjusted.

3. He worked on the brakes.

4. The brakes failed at a critical moment when they should have been in the best condition—if he did a proper job.

5. Mom, a good driver, got no response whatsoever when she stepped on the said adjusted brakes.

6. We dramatically rolled down a steep hill.

7. My grandmother died of injuries as a result. Momma and I could have died, too.

I rest my case.

(Ironically, when Momma died years later, it was in a car that rolled off the road into a deep ravine. Her then-husband landed on top of her and couldn't move. She suffocated before help found them hours later.)

Mom tried to enroll me in the first grade just before I turned six in November, but they wouldn't accept me. When she enrolled me the next year, I played hooky so much, they wouldn't pass me to the next grade.

One side of the room was first grade. The other was second grade. So humiliating to stay on the first-grade side and see all my friends over on the second-grade side. But it settled me down enough that I never failed again.

When I was about eight, we left Mountain View, Wyoming, in the dead of night on a Greyhound bus, owing probably everybody in town some money, and ended up in Ogden, Utah. We lived over a machine shop in a bedbug-infested flophouse while Mom worked in a café next door. I was absolutely no help to Mom, and she had no control over me.

I ran wild.

When she gave me a list of things she needed and some money, I went to the movies instead and spent the rest of the money on snacks. I was crazy about movies, spending all day at the theater, watching the same one over and over again. When the theater closed, I dreaded going home.

Instead, I crawled into the buses around the post office and slept. One night, the weather turned—freezing. I woke up shivering.

Big, soft, fluffy snowflakes fell. I noticed a little red wagon on the sidewalk, full of gunny sacks. I had not heard anyone pulling it, and I saw no one around me or the wagon. Looking back, I believe it might have been the hand of God on the handle.

I excitedly grabbed all the gunny sacks, crawled back into the bushes, wrapped up, and slept warm the rest of the night.

Another time I awoke, lying on a flat cart inside somewhere, wondering where I was. People sat all around me, waiting for me to wake up. I don't know how they got me out of those bushes, carried me inside, and laid me on a mail cart without waking me up.

After asking me who I was and why I was sleeping in the bushes, I told them, "I got lost."

Later, I conveniently remembered where I lived. I hoped that with them accompanying me home, Mom might not give me a whipping. She thanked them graciously, and when they left, I got the whipping I deserved.

But I didn't learn my lesson. I was incorrigible. When Mom sent me to the store, desperately hoping I returned with her grocery items, I fell back to my habitual MO (modus operandi). Again, I would go to a movie, spend all the money, crawl into the bushes, and go to sleep with no remorse.

One morning, I crawled out of the bushes, shivering, and walked with both arms wrapped around myself, trying to warm up. One person in a suit on the gray, predawn streets—and he walked toward me.

Attempting to be cordial, I greeted him. "Good morning, sir." Fine attempt at appearing mature.

He walked right up to me and asked if my name was Tony Hatch.

Surprised, I couldn't even move instinctively. How did he know my name? I tensed up, shaking—although no longer from the morning chill. I hesitated and then replied in the affirmative.

Evidently, Mom reported me missing, and he was searching for me. He did a perfect job of finding me. No telling how many streets he combed before he saw me.

He took me by the shoulder and walked me to the courthouse where there was a juvenile jail and booked me in. Since he was strong, I couldn't break away from him even if I tried. They locked me in a narrow cell by myself on the top floor of the courthouse. I had a bed, a sink, and a commode. Finest facilities I'd ever seen. I loved the commode. And oh yes—a window. With bars.

I could see down and considered escaping, but the height took my breath away! I could stand on a cliff looking over the edge, but standing on the ledge of a tall building terrified me. Fortunately, the bars discouraged me from the initial instinct I'd seen in the movies to tear my sheets into strips and climb out the window to the sidewalk six or seven floors below. I didn't look out the window often. It spooked me.

Every night, two girls periodically came by several times. They opened my little window in the door, where they slipped the food through, and shined a flashlight in to check on me. They laughed and sounded like teenagers, but I don't think they allowed teenagers to work that late at night.

I don't remember eating, but I must have. I was used to eating scraps out of waste baskets and finishing half-drunk bottles of soda water in the trolley station trash cans. The amount of good food people threw away amazed me. Anything they gave me tasted better than remnants. I hated water. Still do. It nauseates me if I drink more than a few swallows.

Two long, lonely weeks passed. They took me to court and took all my mother's custody away from me. A pretty lady drove me in her new little brown coupe to the Robert Shelton foster home in Salt Lake City.

My new foster family were Seventh-Day Adventists. People laughed and pointed fingers at us when we walked to catch the bus for church on Saturdays. I never understood why we went to church on Saturdays. I know now and agree. Even Jesus celebrated the Sabbath on Saturdays!

Mr. Shelton drove a city bus for a living. They had several older daughters, and a son named Bobby, a year or two older than me. My brother, Wayne, and sister, Ramona, were in the home when I got there. My youngest brother, Craig, was placed in a different home. I don't know why.

Bobby and I got along well. We both loved airplanes and made a scrapbook full of photographs we cut out of magazines. We both drew pictures of airplanes, horses, and movie cowboys—Gene Autry, Wild Bill Elliott, Lash LaRue, Hopalong Cassidy, etc.

I especially liked The Durango Kid, because his guns shot the most smoke out of the end of the barrels. I suspect they were putting white powder in the blanks to make it look like smoke.

We always argued about who could draw the best. Bobby thought he could. Course, I **knew** I could. Mrs. Shelton insisted we sit on the edge of the bathtub and wash our feet before we went to bed. I loved to sit or lie on my bed and draw or look at my airplane magazines, even in the daytime.

Mrs. Shelton often walked in and told me, "Get outside and let the stink blow off of you."

A few days before Christmas, the Sheltons gave us all $5 to buy presents when we went to town. I hardly believed it the first time it happened. If I wanted money before, I always had to steal it. We had only one stipulation—we had to spend it on presents for each other, not ourselves. Oh, that was tough.

We could buy a hamburger and a root beer, though. Hamburgers cost only 10¢ or 15¢ back then as I recall. I don't remember cheeseburgers. Maybe no one invented them yet—except in

Dagwood sandwiches. Dagwoods had everything you could imagine on them.

Mom used to call me Wimpy because I loved hamburgers so much. Wimpy was the character in the *Popeye* cartoons who craved hamburgers constantly. I fantasized about having a drawer under my bed filled with hot hamburgers, so I could reach down inside anytime I wanted one.

In those days, department stores had maybe ten or fifteen long tables about six feet wide and ten to twenty feet long, covered with similar items. A girl inside walked back and forth to sell items. A different girl worked at each booth. No shelves. All tabletops with compartments. I loved 'em. I'd walk around, just looking and wishing—and snatching something when the girl got distracted.

One of my chores was taking the trash about fifty yards back to the burn barrel. Most of the time, this chore fell in the darkness of night. I just knew a boogeyman waited there to grab me. I sang loudly and pretty, all the way to the barrels and back, because I didn't believe the boogeyman would get me while I sang prettily.

We had an irrigation ditch I had to cross, and I found an old sheet-metal sign about three feet wide by six feet long lying there. I conceived the idea of rolling it into the shape of a canoe and folding the ends over double about two inches overlapping. I could hammer them down flat with a rock, hoping they would be watertight. I awkwardly rolled the sign into the ditch full of water, and it floated just like I hoped. A tiny bit of water leaked at the folded ends, but nothing I couldn't handle.

I carefully balanced as I stepped inside and knelt. I should have bent the edges down a half-inch overlapping, too. Rather jagged and sharp, they cut my hands in a few places, which I didn't notice at the time, elated with my success in making the canoe.

I could only float short distances, since my canoe was slightly wider than the ditch in a few places. Fences crossed the ditch at both ends, preventing me from canoeing more than thirty or forty yards either way. Besides, I didn't have a paddle. Didn't even think about making one.

That's me! Never think things through to the end. "Up the creek without a paddle."

But it was so simple, and I still think it would be a very marketable project—except with the ends riveted together over a waterproof flat gasket instead of folded over and pounded flat. It's up for grabs, but you can't patent it since I already disclosed it herein.

Besides the boogeyman at the burn barrel, a lion lived under my bed. I never saw him, but I knew he lived there. When I had to use the restroom, I'd wait until I thought he might be asleep, then make a mad dash. The same getting back into bed—in case he woke when I got up.

We lived by a family of Mormons and were not allowed to play together. When we had to walk to catch the school bus, we walked on one side of the road while the Mormons walked on the other. After we got to school, we played together. But after we got off the bus, we went to our respective sides of the road to walk home.

We threw dirt clods back and forth across the road at each other. One day, I picked up a stone about the size of a silver dollar and hit one kid in the temple. It scared me when he dropped like a sack of spuds, flat to the ground.

I thought I killed him

Terrified, I feared they'd try me for murder and then sentence me to the electric chair like in the movies.

I couldn't catch my breath. My lungs felt full, but I still tried to gulp more air. When he got up a little later, I felt relieved.

Short-lived relief, because when Mr. Shelton pulled into the driveway, the mother immediately informed him of the situation. He called all of us boys into the living room and began a methodical interrogation followed by leather punishment. As stated at the beginning of this story, I wanted to lie, but couldn't.

Mom had permission to visit once a month and always bought me airplane magazines to read, which I shared with Bobby. Before long, she remarried and had a baby named Jimmy. At the time, we watched a cartoon character named Jiminy Cricket, and we all called my new brother Jiminy instead of Jimmy.

We dearly loved Jiminy, even though we never met him.

On one of her monthly visits, Mom informed us Jiminy died. She told us her new husband, in a drunken rage, tried to hit her but missed and hit Jiminy instead, killing him.

A few years ago, I got a phone call from a guy named Feril Heaton who told me he believed he was my brother.

I couldn't think straight momentarily, but finally, politely told him, "I think you made an error in your search. I never had a brother named Ferril and don't have any gaps in our family history that I know of."

His story didn't fit. Ironically, I told him about the brother we called Jiminy that my mom's husband tragically killed when he was only a few months old. We ended the conversation with me believing I had convinced him of the error of his research.

He called a few days later and said, "I was adopted, and my name at birth was Jimmy."

The realization hit me like a ton of bricks. Here was my little Jiminy Cricket back from the dead! I was elated.

It seems my mother feared her husband would eventually harm Jimmy, so she gave him to a trusted friend to adopt as her son. He knew early on about the adoption but didn't want to hurt his "adoptive mother" by asking pointed questions.

When he eventually asked about his real parents, she shared with him the facts and helped him find us—with her blessing. A fine woman indeed. God bless her and hers.

Mom never revealed to her abusive husband who she gave Jimmy to. She endured many threats and blows before finally divorcing him.

We invited Jiminy, now Ferril, to an upcoming Hamilton reunion in Robertson, Wyoming. Everybody accepted our brother and his family. We shared many memories and made dozens more. Ferril and his family dropped by to visit me recently, and my family put together a big picnic at Hewlett Park in Granbury. We rented the pavilion for four hours in case it rained, but all went well. Two of Ferril's older granddaughters told us they liked Granbury so much, they intended to move here as soon as they could.

I mentioned that Granbury is the friendliest town I ever lived in, and they said that was their experience, too, so far. I used to carry a stroller in the back of my pickup, and when I unloaded it, two or three people ran up to help me. When I loaded it back up, two or three other people ran up to help me again. I decided right quick I wanted to live here but could not find any place I could afford.

My dad had Shawnee blood coursing through his veins from the Tecumseh tribe in New York. My mother was a quarter Shoshoni Indian with an interest in two acres of Yellow Beads' land on the Wind River Indian Reservation in Wyoming.

About thirty years ago or more, my brother, Wayne, and I received a notice to attend a meeting on the reservation to confirm the accuracy of the records. In that meeting, in listing all the heirs to Yellow Breads' land, we pointed out we had a deceased brother named Jimmy. It wouldn't make any difference since he wouldn't inherit anything. But we didn't want him to be forgotten.

When he finally found his way back into our family, I believe it showed him how much we loved him, even though we thought he died.

The Shelton family had an older married daughter living in New York, and when they learned my dad lived there, too, they had her look him up and inform him where I was. He remarried, drove out to Utah, and adopted me out of the foster home. My mother tried to attend the hearing, but the trolley she was riding wrecked, leaving her with severe injuries. One shoulder remained lower than the other for the rest of her life.

Dad's new wife was named Oleta Zinn. She had been in the Women's Army Service Corp during World War II. She was very good to me and taught me how to make Rice Crispy Cookies, which I dearly loved.

While we lived in Plainview, Texas, Oleta's hometown, I was showing off on the tricky bars after school one day—the bars hung like a ladder overhead. I swung from one rung to the other, like Tarzan, when my hand lost its grip. If fell backward onto my head.

The next thing I remember was waking up, needing to go to the bathroom. We lived on the third floor of an old house, and the bathroom was on the second.

In the dark, I felt my way to find the stairs going down. I kept bumping into things I didn't remember being there. Suddenly, a light clicked on, and Dad and Oleta stood beside me asking if I was alright.

I replied, "Yes."

A long sofa blocked the stairs, confusing me.

They said I came in from school and sat down to supper but said nothing.

I didn't respond to a hand waved in front of my eyes. Gradually, they realized I was unconscious with my eyes open. They put me to bed and pushed the sofa across the stairs to keep me from falling down them.

I told them about falling from the tricky bar but had no idea how I got home.

The next day at school, I asked the kids I was playing with what happened, and they said I just got up and started walking. I walked about five city blocks, across four busy intersections to the correct house, turned in, walked up four steps, climbed up three flights of stairs, sat in my seat at the table, and ate—all while unconscious.

Go figure. I believe we all have a guardian angel that walks with us at least some of the time. He didn't prevent my fall but guided me home, maybe even stopping cars at intersections. I don't know. But I truly believe God had a hand in getting me home safely that day.

I've had similar interventions at other times and other places, but none as dramatic.

Recently, I saw a story about a guy who got beat up and hit his head on the floor, resulting in a concussion. After he got out of the hospital, he realized his whole thinking process was totally different.

I wonder if that's why I became something of a weirdo. I just don't see life, think, feel, or reason like most people do.

Mom later remarried a man named Sam Byrne, a paratrooper, who had just gotten out of a German POW camp. He returned home to Ogden, Utah, after the war. President Roosevelt died while Sam was a prisoner. The German guards told them the U.S. would lose the war, since we didn't have a leader any longer. They evidently didn't understand our concept of a republic government "of the people, by the people, for the people." We always have a leader.

Sam's dad owned a ranch, but Sam didn't want to go back to ranching. I always wondered why. I loved working on a ranch. I have three uncles who own ranches and spent several summers between school terms working on one or another ranch. They always gave me the most fun jobs. At night, they kept one horse in the corral and let the others out into the fields and pastures. My first job was to saddle that horse the next morning and round up the rest of the horses.

I lived in cowboy heaven.

And I loved the other chores, too.

One day a neighboring rancher hired me to help him pull up fence posts and saw them into firewood lengths. His little daughter kept running by and came too close to the big spinning saw blade. He tried to wave her away. His hand went too close to the saw, and I watched in horror when his thumb went flying off.

I finished the rest of the posts myself while his wife took him to the doctor.

Sam chose to stay in Ogden instead of returning to his dad's ranch and drove a taxi for a while. Then he got on the Southern Pacific railroad as a Gandy Dancer, working on the tracks. They called them Gandy Dancers because almost all the tools they used on the tracks were made by the Gandy company. He helped my mom get on her feet and get all her children back except me.

Mom wrote Dad and asked if I could travel from Texas up to Utah and spend the summer with my brothers and sisters. He agreed and bought me a pass on the railroad he worked for.

The train I traveled on went backward from San Angelo to Cheyenne, although I never knew why and couldn't tell the difference. It looked the same to me. Then I rode west from Cheyenne to Evanston.

I met Sam for the first time at the train depot in Evanston, Wyoming, and we drove up to his dad's ranch in Roberton, Wyoming.

I spent three summers working on one or another of my three uncles' ranches in Wyoming. One summer, I was helping drive a herd of cattle up to summer grazing when a breachy cow made a break for it. She took off running for the tall tules. My horse knew his job and pursued instinctively.

I grabbed the saddle horn to stay on with my horse dodging between pines, over fallen trees, when suddenly we started under a big pine bough with the sharp tip of a broken, jagged branch pointing right at my face and coming on fast.

I instinctively dropped my head, and the pointy branch slipped under my jacket collar and down my back, ripping my jacket off in two pieces without even tearing my shirt. I got the cow back into the herd, and my two companions could only stare in amazement at the two pieces of jacket I still wore.

Sam finally worked up to Relief Foreman, working for a month at a time in a different section town so that foreman could take a vacation. We lived in a house-car made out of a converted boxcar with a coal stove and two large water tanks suspended from the ceiling over the stove. It was my job to keep those tanks full with a long hose. We had a shower and plenty of bunks. I loved it.

When we had to move to another railroad section town, a crew would come and slide our stairs up into the "foyer" at the end of the car by the kitchen. We were never allowed to ride inside. We'd catch the 'local' that transported workers free every day one way in the morning and the other way in the evening. When the crew came and drug our stairs out and down, then and only then could we reenter for another month.

One month, we lived on a side track of the trestle at Bagley that crosses the Great Salt Lake. We could lie there at night and listen to the waves splashing against the pilings of the trestle. Hypnotic and wonderful, it created the perfect sound for sleeping.

We could hear other trains coming down the tracks and always wondered if they were on the right track. Then they'd flash by us, and we could see out of our windows directly into their lighted windows about two feet away. We wondered about them—where they were going. It was fun.

Strangely, at times, I experienced a weird time phenomenon where, for a split second, time froze. I could see their faces in detail, but only for an instant. Then everybody became a blur again. Possible for them to see into our windows, especially when we had a light on, too, they didn't expect to see anything. Even if they stared out their windows, they didn't have time to focus on anything close like we did.

One day, my grandfather Rob Roy McGregor Hamilton dropped in on us, intending to stay a week. The very next morning he was ready to leave. He could hear trains all night long and feared they were on our track. He never came back to visit.

Oh! Did I say I loved it?

We had to drive about thirty miles on a one-lane rutted dirt road to buy groceries and supplies. We often stopped and treated ourselves to a store-bought meal with a malt or milkshake.

One day at a curio shop in Wendover, Utah, Sam ran into an old war buddy.

He said, "Hey, I want you to meet my family." Sam called us kids over. "This is Tony, my oldest."

He went right down the line introducing ALL of us as "his" kids, although none were biologically except Sammie, the youngest.

I could hardly believe what I heard. In that moment, I sincerely felt he chose to adopt me concretely, although nothing legal transpired.

Later, Sam opened up to me about his war experiences. At first, he didn't hate Germans. His buddy's mom always sent cookies he shared with Sam until he got killed. Then Sam's hatred of Germans began. A Tiger tank chased him once, but he got away. He had been dropped behind enemy lines. He and his buddies hid in a haystack, and the Germans walked around, jabbing their bayonets into the stack. They unwittingly stuck one guy's leg, but he gritted his teeth and didn't cry out.

They finally set the haystacks on fire, which forced Sam and the others out. The enemy took them to a prisoner of war camp where they kept him until the war ended. At home, Sam often woke in the middle of the night, screaming.

He gradually became a role model for me, and I came to love him as a father figure. Partly because of his example, I easily accepted my wife's two sons from a previous marriage when I got married. I also consider a mother's children to come from her very soul. They are truly in the purest sense of the word part of her. Children "come with the territory." If you love one, you love 'em all.

One day, Sam saw me carrying railroad ties around and making forts with them. He decided I was strong enough to hold down a full-time job. He got me on at a salt plant in Saline, Utah, where they kilned salt from Great Salt Lake and bagged it in 100-pound sacks. They required a social security number, but I was two years too young. Mom or Sam scratched enough of the 1935 year off to convert it to 1933. That resulted in my getting a social security number.

When I actually retired, they told me I could have drawn Social Security two years earlier. Wow. I wish I realized that sooner.

I loved working at the salt plant. They had a big, long barrel about eight feet in diameter that slowly rotated, and a big jet engine shot a long blast of heat down through the rotating barrel to dry the salt from the lake. The salt slowly moved down the barrel and sifted through decreasing-sized screens into containers below.

Sometimes, the salt melted from the heat and stuck to the inside of the barrel. Then they sent me up to a platform beside the rotating barrel, and I used a sledgehammer to pound the melted salt loose.

I fantasized I was John Henry, the steel-driving man. Every day, I had to shower off crusted salt from all over my body and face. We had to put each bag on a conveyor belt down to a boxcar, carry it to the end of the car, and stack them about five deep.

I always bragged and bet the other two guys I could carry three of those 100-pound bags to the end of the car and stack them on top. I did it too, but won't ever do it again. I almost did myself in.

Sam always let me keep the money I earned, but one day, he came to me with a request.

My brother, Wayne, had ruptured his appendix. He needed to be driven on a one-lane winding pothole-filled road about 30 miles to the highway and into Wendover, Utah, for an operation. We learned the hard way not to run over dead jackrabbits on the road because their bones were hard and brittle. They could puncture our threadbare tires. Same asked me if he could borrow money to pay for Wayne's operation. I could in no way refuse that request. I never considered asking for that money back.

Another time, my kid sister, Sammie, playing with matches, caught her rayon gown on fire and burned most of the skin off her tummy. I had to hold her gently on my lap in the back seat, trying to hypnotize her pain away on the way to Wendover again.

I had to quit my salt-plant job to start the eighth grade in Ogden. I've always been something of an actor. Different groups got me to act in skits in the auditorium. Then the drama class came and asked me to accept the lead role in a play, *Starlight, Starbright.* They planned to perform it for the city.

Flattered, I said yes, even though I wasn't in the class. Teachers let me out of my other classes when we rehearsed. At one point, I was expected to kiss the heroine, who was a kind of prima donna. She was beautiful, but I refused to kiss her, and she slapped my face. I agreed to kiss her in the actual play.

Then came the night of our performance. I don't remember a solitary thing about that night!

The next day, the instructor called a meeting in the auditorium to review our performances. He reamed everybody out pretty good, so I wasn't expecting a good review. I braced myself.

He said, "Tony Hatch, you are a natural actor. I worried about whether you were really going to kiss her. Then you scooted over closer to her, and then I started worrying about just how far you were gonna go."

I wish I could remember it.

Since then, I was sought out to play the lead in other skits and plays in other schools. I enjoyed acting.

One night, I pedaled Wayne on my handlebars, coming down a long, steep street two blocks from the traffic light at Broadway. I realized how much fun it would be to back up the hill, time the traffic light at the bottom, and go flying through the four-lane intersection just when all the cars stopped.

I made three practice runs and decided to go for it.

Just as I approached the light at maybe 200 mph, I realized some cross traffic had paced the lights, too, so they hit the intersection just as it turned green for them. If I tried to stop then, I'd probably go down and slide into the middle of the intersection. So I went for broke and pedaled even faster.

I easily beat all the oncoming cars on my left and the first car in the third lane on my right but hit the car in the fourth lane. Wayne flew off the and went running up the street yelling his leg was broken. My front wheel was twisted 90 degrees sideways. A Greyhound bus stopped. People bailed out, trying to catch Wayne. Others tried to wrestle me into a car to take me to the hospital or something.

I finally got my front wheel twisted straight and jumped back on my bike and caught up with Wayne. He jumped back on my handlebars, and we raced for home. The cowboy hat I wore never fell off my head. I thought the movie cowboys were so fake because they never lost their hats in a fight. Once again, I was proven wrong.

We never said a word when we got home. Mom said she knew something bad happened, because she never heard us so quiet.

When I started high school, I attended the closest one, 70 miles away in Montello, Nevada. Sam rented a small cabin for ten dollars a month. Wayne and I rode the 'local' home every week to get supplies for the next week.

Mr. Martin, the principal and instructor, watched for the local winding down the mountains every Friday afternoon. Then he shooed us out of the school to catch it on time. We caught the local every Sunday morning to take us back to Montello.

One winter morning, we couldn't get in the door. Something blocked it. I went around to peek in the kitchen window and saw a sheet of ice on the floor, blocking the door. I crawled through a window and used an axe to chop out the ice and open the door. I drilled several small holes in the floor to let the melted water out.

I left the water faucet dripping slightly, as advised. But the drain iced shut inside and forced the dripping water to fill the sink and overflow onto the floor, where it froze solid about an inch thick.

With no parents around, all the boys gathered at our cabin after school to smoke. I did all the cooking and invented several concoctions the guys tried. I invented chili mac long before it showed up on commercial menus in cafes and restaurants. Even called it Chilimac.

I also invented what I called butter-bathed pancakes, which no one has copied yet to my knowledge. I still prefer them. I use a thin, almost watery batter and fry them only on one side. Bubble holes hold butter, syrup, honey, etc.

The boys mentioned all my concoctions, including lightning cake with merengue frosting to their mothers. They invited me to submit a cake for a raffle they were about to have. It embarrassed me, and I declined. I should have at least thanked them for inviting me. It's one of my deepest regrets that I wasn't man enough to accept their sweet offer. I know they would have created a special category so I could win. Alas.

My best friend was Sterling White. We started rodeoing together, and he invited me to stay at his dad's ranch, so I'd ride with him after school.

He had a girlfriend in town he liked to visit for a couple of hours sometimes after school. Then he dropped by the cabin, and we headed for the Bar O Ranch. His dad, Bishop—Bish for short, said he named it the Bar O because he had to borrow so much to buy it.

One night, It began to snow before we left. Halfway home, we couldn't see the one-lane dirt road any more. But we came across a set of tracks we assumed knew the road, so we followed them until we saw another set. We realized we just followed our tracks around and around. We backtracked until we saw where our track first joined in and backtracked back into town, spending the night at our cabin.

Another time, when we headed out, we had to run about a mile beside the railroad tracks, which sat about four or five feet higher than our road. In the dark, we turned left to cross the tracks. Only then could we see a slow-moving train rolling along the tracks. We didn't have any brakes on that old Model T Sterling's dad bought for us to go to school.

Sterling did a fantastic job of gearing down to slow us, but it wasn't enough. We gently hit a moving car, and it stopped us. We jumped out to pull the car away, but another car caught it and drug it a little farther.

We backed off completely, but as the caboose went by, it snagged the Model T again, and the crew inside the train shined bright spotlights at us. We knew when they got to town, we'd be reported. Nothing to do but wait and watch as a car headed out of town on its way to the scene of the crime.

The sheriff drove up with the depot manager, both who had a reputation of being hard nosed about everything. After we explained the situation, they both laughed. We hoped for a happy ending.

The depot manager said if the caboose had been damaged, we'd have to pay for repairs. But it didn't have any damage. They called us the gold-brick twins. Not sure why, but they always treated us friendly after that.

At the end of the summer, I wrote to my dad and asked if I could stay with my brothers and sisters permanently. He hesitated but finally agree. He came to visit me from San Angelo every few months until he died.

One time, I had moved and failed to send him my new address. He drove to Fort Worth anyway, trying to find me by slowly driving around neighborhoods and looking for a clue. When he saw an old-timey New York style push vendor caret in the front yard, he said he felt I had something to do with it. He walked up and knocked on the door. You could have knocked me over with a feather when I recognized my dad standing there.

Some kids never had a dad in their lives. I'm very fortunate to have two wonderful dads in my life!

I love both equally but for different reasons.

My thanks to the Robert Shelton family for treating me like a human being and making me feel at home. Some kids in foster care don't have it as good as I did.

"I don't thank God for the good things you do; I thank God for making people like you."

The End...

or not

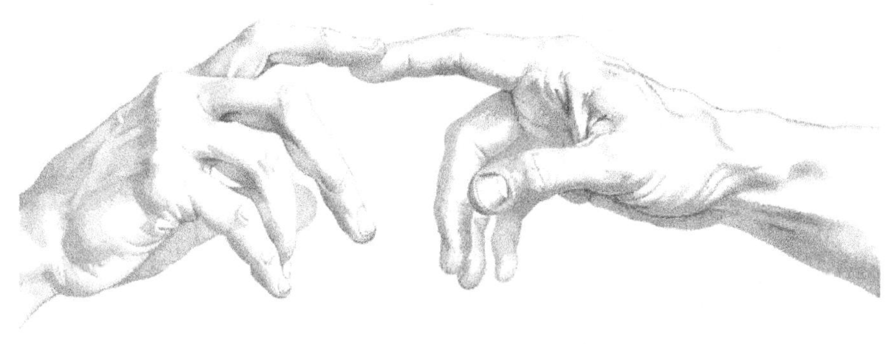

Something More

J.W. Dickson

We have studied this life,
the road we're on.
The crossroads and the roads less traveled.
And we ask in our search,
Lord, is there something more?

Many have searched for the reasons of this life's existence.
Its purpose, our duty,
astounded by the facets of its beauty.
And they ask in their search,
Lord, is there something more?

Some have sought solutions to riddles and rhymes,
Scientists and doctors police crimes
Against this world and nature's tragedies.
And they ask in their quest,
Lord, is there something more?

Then as winter turns into spring and celebrates life,
as every newborn begins to thrive,
Parents shout, Thank you, Lord,
there is something more!

At every new scientific discovery,
from wheels to walks on the moon,
as every lost soul finally comes home,
angels shout.

As every sorrow is turned to singing,
And those who mourn begin to dance,
as every loneliness is filled with love,
hearts shout,
Thank you, Lord,
there is something more

The most important lessons I learned in life have come from the Lord. God is good. When I listened, I knew what to do next. Seek wisdom and knowledge, like silver and gold. Be honest, trustworthy, ethical, humble, loving, kind, faithful, courageous, creative, righteous, peaceful, spiritual, and inventive.

JWD,
hopeful, thankful and blessed

The Carpenter*

Lisa Bell

The carpenter ran his hand across the smooth surface of the table. He smiled, wiped the sweat from his brow, and walked to the water bucket for a drink. As he dipped a cup, he looked down at his strong feet, wiggled his toes, and chuckled. He curled his toes, and the chuckle turned into a laugh so deep and strong a young man passing by stopped.

"What are you laughing about, you old goat?"

"Old? Who are you calling old, boy? But if you must know, sometimes moving my toes just gets the better of me. I can't help but burst out laughing."

"You are strange, *old* man. And I'm not a boy." He held out his hand. "I'm Paul—named after some preacher my mother heard many years ago."

The carpenter shook Paul's hand and looked across the road at a tree where an old man sat beneath it, begging. "Do you see that old man over there?"

The young man shrugged. "Sure, he's there every day. Sometimes I toss a coin at him or share a piece of bread."

"You know that used to be my spot," said the carpenter.

Paul cocked an eyebrow. "You? Why? I mean you are kind of old, but you look strong and healthy."

"Yes, but it wasn't always so. At about your age, I spent every day under that tree. Often, I whittled away wood or bone to make small useful objects. Spoons, bowls—things of that sort." He tapped his temple. "See, my brain worked fine when talking to my hands. My feet and legs? Eh, not so much. From the moment of my birth, my feet never worked right."

An incredulous look passed over Paul's face, and he looked down at the carpenter's feet. "They looked fine now. And they obviously work because you're standing on them."

"Ah, that's why moving my toes makes me laugh." He wiggled them for effect and continued. "One day, while I sat under that tree, two men stood nearby talking. One asked if the other heard about Paul and Barnabas and all the miracles they did. I tell you, my ears perked up at that word miracles." He sat on a bench, patting it as an invitation for Paul to join him. "I listened to those two men for what seemed an hour, never tiring of the stories they shared with each other. I was a bit skeptical. But for the first time in my life, I dared hope for feet that could move."

Paul tilted his head slightly, his eyebrows rising, but one eye narrowed. "So, what happened?"

"A few days later, a crowd gathered around me. To my surprise and delight, the man Paul stood across the street—not far from where we are now." Warmth spread over the carpenter as he smiled. "He spoke of someone named Jesus. Every word he said amazed me. I wanted to know more about the gospel he shared, so I listened." The carpenter shifted his feet.

"Without warning, he locked eyes with me. 'Stand up on your feet!' he commanded."

Paul's eyes widened. "What did you do?"

"Oh, I did not stand. I jumped to my feet and took the first steps of my life."

Paul placed a hand on his cheek. "That's impossible. How do you walk when you've never taken a step or had someone teach you?"

The carpenter shrugged. "I'm not sure. Never asked that question." He stroked his thick beard. "Hmmm. I suppose when the name of Jesus healed me, He somehow gave me the knowledge and wisdom to walk. I mean what good would it be to have healed feet and still not be able to use them? Thank you for asking that question. I never thought about that before."

Paul stood and placed a hand on the carpenter's shoulder and walked away, leaving him deep in thought.

That night, Paul sat with his mother and father. He asked about his namesake.

His mother beamed. "I hoped someday you would ask. Let me tell you about the day I met Paul. I gathered with a group of people while he shared the gospel of Jesus. Then he healed a man—lame from birth."

The young man clasped his hands in front of him. "I know that man, Mother. In fact, I met him today. I thought maybe he made up his healing story."

"No," his father said. "I was there. So many times, we saw that young man sitting under the tree, carving things but unable to use his feet at all. When Paul the Apostle told him to stand, he jumped high into the air and landed on solid feet that held strong. To our amazement, he walked through the crowd and all around us. Impossible but true."

His mother nodded. "Others believed Paul and Barnabas to be gods, but we knew better. It wasn't the first time we heard him speak. As travelers, we heard of Jesus before that day. Seeing the miracle affirmed what we already believed. And that's when we decided to name you after the Apostle."

The young Paul breathed deeply and exhaled. "When I talked to the old man today, he explained how he could walk. But he didn't know how he understood the process of walking. Can you?"

His mother shrugged. "Well, I suppose if God is powerful enough to heal someone, how can we question whether He's powerful enough to teach them a simple thing like walking?

Paul smiled then. "I think you're right. Even a child must learn how to walk, but the old carpenter just knew. How else can you explain it? If God heals someone, why would he leave them in a state where they had to go back to their infirmity? Tell me more about Paul... and this Jesus you serve."

*Based on Acts 14:8-19

Joy in Obedience

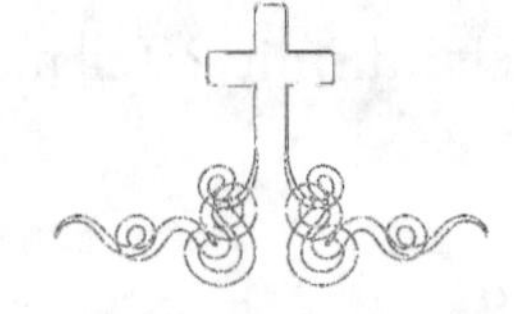

Vicki Woodson

"If you keep my commands, you will remain in my love,
just as I have kept my Father's commands and remain in
his love. I have told you this so that my joy may be in you
and that your joy may be complete."
John 15: 10-11 NIV

The moon cast long shadows across my room as I tossed and turned at 2:00 a.m. Sleep remained elusive. I sought God's will to write a story for an anthology. A sudden inspiration struck me, and an idea formed in my mind. Through writing, I've learned to appreciate the intricate details and quiet moments that filled this journey with joy and self-understanding. Instead of dwelling on the negative, I focused on laughter, joy, and celebrating small victories. Joy and obedience were the answer to my prayer.

The Heights Church, my place of worship, was holding its annual twenty-one days of prayer, and the quiet reverence of the building filled the air. On that evening, Pastor Daniel invited those seeking a special anointing for their hands to come forward for prayer. I went, believing in the power of laying hands on the sick for healing—a special anointing seemed even better. Pastors Daniel and Ashley prayed for everyone, including me. Unexpectedly, God allowed me to use this anointing to pray for someone a couple of days later.

On that chilly night, I pulled into my driveway. The icy wind hastened my steps as I exited the car and hurried to the house. The day couldn't be over fast enough for me. It included cleaning two houses, so I intended to get inside the warm house, have dinner, and rest. My comfortable couch with a cozy throw beckoned to me. Wearily, I sat down, took off my shoes, covered myself with a blanket, and thought about dinner when my cell interrupted me.

My sister and I have lived next door for over fifteen years. Despite difficulties and trials, we love each other and would do anything for one another. She is usually very active, often seen working in her yard or shopping. That night, her voice hoarse, she struggled to speak and coughed as she gave me the details of her last few days. She had visited the doctor twice in two weeks. Eyes closed, I listened to her describe sleepless nights, a stuffy nose, chest congestion, breathing problems, and fatigue.

"Didn't the doctor give you any medicine to treat the symptoms?" I asked when she paused for breath.

Yes, but they weren't helping. Only steroids provided any relief. Her physician wouldn't give her more because of her osteoporosis, but agreed to if she insisted. She chose not to, which resulted in the doctor prescribing more of the same ineffective medication, and she returned home. I could hear the tears as she voiced her dread for another night without sleep.

Had she received prayer at her church?

Nope. She hadn't been to church or anywhere at all in three weeks.

If you can't tell already, I didn't want to go out and pray for my sister. God knew I was tired, and besides that, the frigid air made me want to stay right there—under my warm blanket.

She only lives next door, but I would have to put my shoes back on, a coat, brace for the icy wind, and trudge over to her house.

Lord, do I have to?

He reminded me of the special anointing on my hands. Would I be obedient? He answered it was my decision.

Yes, I would be obedient. I told her about my pastors praying over my hands for a special anointing. Did she want me to come over and pray for her? Of course, she said yes. Wouldn't you if you were a believer and modern medicine proved ineffective? Furthermore, she would walk over to my house. Now I really felt ashamed for even hesitating to pray for her. What sibling would I be if I let my sick sister walk over to my house?

With my scriptures in hand, I asked God for the words to pray over my sister, walked over to her house, knocked on her door, and stepped inside. The smell of Vicks hung in the room. Her face was puffy and nose red from blowing it all day. She sat in her recliner, hunched over, with her medicine and tissues next to her.

I read this verse to her.

"And these signs will accompany those who believe; In my name, they will cast out demons; they will speak in new tongues; They will pick up snakes with their hands; and when they drink deadly poison, it will not hurt them; they shall place hands on sick people; and they will get well." (Mark 16: 17-18 NIV).

As a believer, I have been called to lay hands on the sick. In obedience to that word, I put my hand on her shoulder and commanded the symptoms to go in the Name of Jesus. I told her God meant her to be well. She is a child of the King and Jesus paid the price for her healing.

After I finished praying over her, I explained that if the symptoms tried to come back, God gave her the authority to resist them in Jesus' name. Nothing seemed to have changed, but I had been obedient, so I went back home.

While at a client's home the following day, I returned my sister's missed call. She explained it was a butt dial, something she does often.

We didn't discuss the previous evening, but I thought she sounded better. Didn't she? I resolved to ring back after work.

On my way home, impatient, I rang back.

"Well, are all the symptoms gone? You sound better."

"Oh, yes, I'm much better. The coughing tried to come back during the night, but didn't last long. I slept longer and woke up feeling much improved. I'm out shopping." Her voice, clear, confident, and happy, spoke volumes.

For those who don't know my sister, shopping is her superpower. She has a gift for always remembering what everyone needs and finding the perfect present. Now, I can already picture my brother-in-law's eye roll, but she's always been this way, even back when we were kids playing in the backyard. Why am I telling you about her shopping? It brings her joy, especially when getting that perfect gift for loved ones, and God gave her the strength to get back out there. Her desire to give to others is one of her joys, and God used me as a conduit to heal her and help her get back to it.

Joy, a spiritual force, washed over me. My joy is to do the will of the Father. We can have joy in good or bad times. How? Genuine joy is in our salvation, and no one can steal it. Obedience to our Father's will determines the outcome of our endeavors.

I didn't have to choose to pray for my sister, but it was important for her health for me to do so. Every day, God allows us to choose to obey that inner voice of His Holy Spirit. Big choices, little ones, each set us on a course to do the will of the Father. Obedience is not duty or obligation, but an adventure in stepping out into the path God has called me. As I set my face to do His will and remain in His love, joy will be in me, and it will be complete. Each day, I want to look for an opportunity to be a blessing to others. Sometimes it's when I am tired, but God always gives me strength. After all, the joy of the Lord is my strength, right?

Lord, help me always to be obedient, to step out boldly and fulfill your calling, no matter the challenges.

The Leaf

Cynthia Tippett

At an outside memorial for my granddaughter
Cynthia Tippett

A leaf, swirling, swirling,
Red and gold, twirling, twirling,
Gently floating, alluring, alluring,
To my lap, enduring, enduring.

Her angel has touched, sweeping, sweeping,
To a throng, weeping, weeping,
A silence ensued, sweetly, sweetly.

Awaken! She shouts, cheering, cheering
For her good life, endearing, endearing,
And her angel appears, nearing, nearing.

Then she embraces us, loving, us,
Hovers us, covers us,
Swirling, swirling, twirling, twirling!

Saintly Sinner*

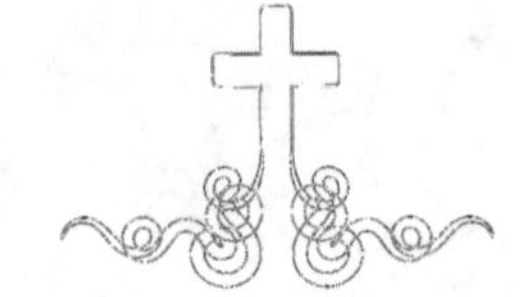

JuneAnn Brown

Ruth Ann got in her car and drove away. Away from her home, her husband, the church, and this town. Tom didn't want her to leave, but he wouldn't think about her, anyway.

When she got to the interstate, she breathed a sigh of relief. The excitement built as she journeyed toward a different life. She was ready. Free. She had missed time in the city. Her foot stepped on the gas.

Ruth Ann maneuvered the traffic in the big city. Hotel check-in complete, she went to her room and waited for her bags. Sitting on the bed and planning the next four days was the best part. She would be a new woman. She couldn't wait.

Different name, different clothes, different attitude. She smiled.

"Yes. Freedom."

She hated being just the preacher's wife. She also hated the dowdy clothes Tom picked out for her. Her plans for the next four days didn't include her preacher-husband. A strange feeling weighted down her chest. She sneezed.

"Oh no. I hope I'm not getting a cold," she said to the empty room.

A knock sounded on the door.

"Luggage," announced the bellman.

She opened the door, and the young man brought in her bags. He smiled. Then he turned toward the door to leave. She barely got a bill into his hand before he was out the door.

Ruth Ann opened the luggage and hung her clothes, putting personal things in the drawers. She could already feel the change coming over her. Nothing calmed her as much as when she came to the city. With everything put away, she changed her clothes, got her purse, and headed to the elevator. She walked purposefully, head lifted, shoulders back, hips moving with each step. Plenty of time to eat before she started conducting business that night. Yes, she was beginning the transformation—becoming Roxy in the big city.

Ruth Ann played the dutiful preacher's wife. She could still hear the hurtful whisperings of those church ladies. But this was her real life, here in the city. Ruth Ann stepped out of the hotel. Freedom saturated her skin. She loved it. She watched the people as they walked by. Did they see her?

Yes. They weren't ignoring her, and she loved the attention. She looked at her reflection in the store windows. What fun. Maybe she did look mousey at church. Roxy always looked better than Ruth Ann. She was smarter than Ruth Ann and sure had more personality.

Ruth Ann felt more like Roxy. She was in control. People knew her, and she had things to do.

Roxy walked three blocks to her favorite restaurant, where the hostess showed her to the corner booth—her favorite. The Sugar Shack was mainly a burger cafe with hot soups and homemade pies. The lights glowed soft, providing a cozy atmosphere in the place. The cool air inside boosted her appetite. The waitstaff knew and welcomed her. Before she asked, the server brought her a hot cup of coffee.

"Here ya go. Cream and sugar, just the way you like it."

"These strangers know me better than my husband does," she muttered to herself.

Her burger and fries arrived, and the waitress topped off her coffee.

"You haven't been here in a while. We miss you," she said.

"Thank you," replied Roxy. "You really have no idea how I miss being here."

Roxy sat for a while, sipping coffee, thinking about all the times she sat in that booth. As she considered her life, a small laugh escaped her bright-red lip sticked mouth. Tom didn't have a clue where she was or what she was doing. Free, because Tom hated her family and would never call any of them to check on her. Free to do whatever she wanted. Roxy paid the bill and walked back to the hotel room.

"I'm not feeling any better." She said, rubbing her chest.

Roxy was anxious to put on her real clothes and venture out. With every garment she put on, she changed into Roxy. She looked at herself in the mirror and admired the transformation. Ruth Ann no longer existed. Hell-lo Roxy. Her life and her character changed completely.

As she left the hotel, she didn't turn right toward the front but headed left to go out the back. She loved life in the big city with an auburn bobbed wig, black tight leather pants, a black leather jacket, and black boots. She loved putting on her leathers. Her makeup completed the transformation, she felt whole, complete. Roxy was real! As she took the short walk to the abandoned building, the stench overwhelmed her for a moment.

One-by-one, her friends saw her, happy to call out a welcome.

"Roxy!" her friends shouted.

The excitement built. "Roxy's here."

"Hey Rox!"

"Welcome back. It's good to see you."

"It's about time!" said the old grouch who was neither old nor a grouch. A slight smile crossed his face.

Everybody stopped what they were doing, turned, and welcomed her. Roxy got caught up in the excitement and forgot about the stink and trash in the old building.

"Where's Chester?" she asked.

Everyone grew quiet for a couple of seconds before Hollywood said, "He passed last week."

Complete silence fell on the room for a while, then he said in his low, soft growl, "He was beat up real bad, stabbed in the heart by a couple of guys that were robbin' him. We called the police, but he was already gone." Hollywood sniffed. "We watched from the top of that old building, then I came back. We scatter pretty much in the evenings, cause that's when the cops come to ask us questions. I handled it. Talked to the Blue. Answered all their questions."

No one added to the story.

Then Roxy said, "He was one of a kind. We'll miss him."

"He was a good man," said Crazy Mary. "Yes, he was. A good man. Yip, good man."

Crazy Mary never knew how to stop talking once she said something. She walked away mumbling, "Good man. Yes, he was a good man. Good, good, man. Dead man."

It hurt Roxy's heart to think of Chester's last moments on earth. She remembered the first time she talked to him about Jesus.

"Is everyone ok with a prayer for Chester?" Heads bowed in submission.

"I'll pray for Chester." Hollywood, who seldom spoke or volunteered for anything, prayed in a loud voice. "Dear Lord, we are here to remind you to take special care of our brother Chester. We needed him here, but I guess you needed him more. God rest his soul. Amen."

A loud chorus of "amen" came from the crowd.

Hollywood acquired his name from the glamor pictures he sketched of the women walking by. When they saw their pictures, they were willing to pay a rather high price for the charcoal portrait.

Roxy said, "OK dear friends. I need a report on what's happening around here."

Crazy Mary started the conversation. "Been raped four times. My checks have been stolen twice, and Oscar stole my shoes!" This was the same line she used every time someone asked about her.

"Mary, have you reported this?"

"Hellfire, no! Name me one thang the Blues would do 'cept waste my time. The Blues. Waste. It's a waste. Waste of time. It's a waste," she muttered.

"OK, who needs anything?"

"I need socks."

"I need deodorant."

"I want cookies."

"A coat."

"Gloves. Got any blankets?"

They kept calling out requests. Roxy wrote each need down. She stayed a while and chatted with each person, catching up on their lives. They laughed and talked until they noticed the sun going down. Roxy stood and asked everyone to bow their heads. She offered prayers for their days to be blessed, for their health and safety, and finally for their souls.

"I'll be back tomorrow," she said, getting up and navigating through the homeless people she held so dearly. They knew she would be back. They also knew several men would follow her back to the hotel to make sure she was safe.

"Bye angel. Be careful going back."

"We love you!"

"Shut your mouth bi..." hollered Crazy Mary."

"I love you, too, Mary," replied Roxy softly, and she did love her. She loved them all. They accepted her. They were her family—the one God gave her. But there was that strange feeling deep in her chest.

Roxy had been coming there, doing the Lord's work for about ten years. She did other things for them—writing letters to family or driving them to doctor and dental appointments. They hadn't accepted her as the church lady, but as Roxy, she was one of them. No questions asked.

Returning to the hotel, she used the back door and elevator, tired and sad. Sad for the plight of the homeless. Sad for Chester, who was now gone—one of many she remembered. Her heart was so burdened. She sat on the end of the bed with her head in her hands and wept. She had been doing this for so long. But nothing changed, except for more homeless people and more police to chase them away and throw their meager belongings in the trash.

She took off her wig and clothes, got in the shower, and stayed until the water cooled. Roxy put her gown on and crawled into bed.

Tomorrow.

Roxy got up early, drove to Walmart, shopped, then loaded the supplies in the car and drove back to the crumbling, smelly building where her friends lived. Her thoughts turned back to the church and the ladies.

She always felt so alone in church.

"I don't think even God knows I'm there." She said to herself. "Those goody-two-shoes wouldn't do anything for anyone except bake for church suppers just to receive compliments on their cooking."

That's what they lived for. Cooking and gossiping and condemning Ruth Ann—who they did not know.

Roxy never felt alone with her homeless family. There was always laughter and love. She smiled. After handing out her purchases, she sat for hours with them talking, eating lunch, spending time with her people. This family that made her blossom into the woman she wanted to be. They gave her courage to face her life back home.

She went to her hotel room and lay on the bed. She thought about the people living in the abandoned building. Each had a story. They had mothers and brothers, and families. They had a former life somewhere. She closed her eyes and prayed out loud for each of them as tears slowly fell. She loved them all. Her family.

She had spent four days away, and as she packed her suitcases, she realized Roxy was leaving. Ruth Ann walked out the front door of the hotel, got in her car, and headed home.

The strange feeling in her chest returned. It frightened her. Ruth Ann thought about her life while she drove the familiar route home.

"Yes," she said out loud. "It is time for a talk with Tom."

She had to tell him how she felt in the city—tell him about her homeless family and how they accepted her. And how she loved them. Ruth Ann was tired of hiding her passion for the homeless. He had to understand this was her ministry, her calling. Tom made her into his version of a preacher's wife, and she allowed him to change her.

Suddenly, she understood the feeling deep inside. A whisper from God! Jesus was calling her, willing to take on her burdens. He was always there. She could actually hear His words. Why hadn't she listened?

"I'm listening now, Lord."

He said, "Why haven't you called on me to help you? You know my love for you is greater than your confusion. I have taken every step with you. I have always been with you and given you a mission. It isn't the homeless. Go where I led you—where you started. I will be there. The ladies are waiting for you to lead them. Your husband is waiting for you to take charge of your life. Never forget you are my child."

In a flash, that strange feeling disappeared. God spoke to her. She listened. And she changed.

Ruth Ann rolled her window down, felt the air, and smiled. She knew what she had to do. She was going home. Roxy was gone for good. Ruth Ann was in charge.

"Thank you, Lord."

She pressed the gas pedal harder and raced to her true calling.

*What then shall we say
to these things? If God is for us,
who is against us?
(Romans 8:31 NASB)*

Giants in the Land

Christine Kohler

I weed my daughters' garden
to pay penitence for their sins.
Giants in the land,
bastards of fallen angels,
trampling grapes of wrath.

Briars, brambles, crown of thorns,
once a land of milk and honey.
I prick my fingers,
smear the blood,
curse the weeds that choke the fruit.

Labor long, painful pangs—
tears and sweat mingle water and blood.
Who will redeem my daughters and me?
Who will bare our crown of thorns?

Who will pay penitence for our sins?
Who will drive the bastard giants away?
Restore the land to milk and honey?
Hurry, Yeshua, we await.

Meet the Authors

Authors listed in this section contributed one or more pieces to this anthology. Their names appear in alphabetical order. Enjoying learning more about each of these writers. Encourage them by leaving a review on wherever you purchase books. Reviews go a long way to help authors succeed. We appreciate you, our readers. Without you, out words have little meaning.

Lisa Bell has written hundreds of articles, several nonfiction books, contributed to anthologies, including three Chicken Soup for the Soul editions, plus three novels (and counting). Retired editor of NOW Magazines, LLC. and published author, Lisa provides freelance services for authors, leads three writing groups, and serves on the panel for The Writers View.

Lisa lives in Granbury, TX where she enjoys crafting, sewing, reading, volunteering in the community, and spending time with her daughters and grandchildren.

Mary-margaret Belota is a born and reared Texan, a graduate of Texas Wesleyan College (now University), and a retired elementary school music teacher. She began writing poetry in childhood, later expanding into essays and short stories. She has four volumes of poetry in publication, with a fifth volume scheduled for release in the fall of 2025. Mary-margaret also enjoys taking photographs to go along with her poetry.

Born in Oklahoma. JuneAnn Grider Brown grew up in McGregor, Texas (grade-school years) and Waco, Texas (high-school years). She says, "I've made a lot of wonderful friends in my many travels."

Her writing career took a magical turn when her friend, Dee Dee Ward, encouraged her to write.

"I was hooked and spent all my free time writing and enhance the professionalism of my first novel, which is almost complete. Stay tuned. There's more to come."

Janet Dickson, a rancher, writer, and renovator, based her life and work on faith, prayer, and perseverance. A retired reading teacher and lifelong learner, she finds grace in the ordinary—the worn fence, the open sky, the quiet strength of restoration. Her *Rockbridge* series weaves together faith, community, and redemption, written for dreamers who dare, guardians who pray, and warriors who believe that even broken things can shine again beneath the wide and merciful light.

Tony Hatch is an American singer, songwriter, musician born in Mountain View, Wyoming during the Great Depression. The cowboy life initially captured most of his imagination, but the railroad also shared a dominant influence as Tony reached his teen years. He served in the US Navy in 1950s, learned electronics, and developed his musical style. Tony now enjoys preserving stories from his life and encourages everyone to write their memories.

Christine Kohler is a former journalist, teacher, and writing instructor. *Silent No More* (Wipf and Stock, 2024) is her debut poetry collection, and her 18th book. Kohler is best known as the author of *No Surrender Soldier* (Simon & Schuster, 2014). Parkland College, Illinois, named Kohler a Notable Alumni. Her journalism degree is from the University of Hawaii. Kohler now resides with her husband in Texas.

(Photo by Double Knot Photography.)

Becky Kubiak lives in Texas where she enjoys spending time with family and friends. She supports her local live production theatre and writes stories that include a sense of humor.

Barbara Boothe Loyd earned her BFA in Art History and Literature from the University of Maryland campus in Germany. She taught art to students in first through twelfth grades and adults. She is an award-winning painter, as well as a published writer and poet.

Barbara displays her works in local, regional, national, and international exhibitions.

Graphic designer, homeschool teacher, avid dancer and more, Sarah Olson writes short pieces from her mother's heart, which she shares on Substack. Sarah joined our writers' group with the beginnings of a book and continues working on that project.

She lives in Texas with her husband and three beautiful children.

Native Texan, Wanda Strange resides in Bluff Dale with her husband (since 1969) and daughter. She devotes time to reading, writing, and volunteering in her church and community. She loves music, books, and time with family and friends. Retired, a love of oncology inspires her to encourage patients, caregivers, and colleagues. Her passion for people motivates stories of God's faithfulness. Her published works include *Legacy: Memories, Mysteries, Musing; Emerging from the Crucible: Enduring God's Refining Fire; and Abundant Heart: A Five-Year Gratitude Journal.*

wstrange0306@gmail.com
https://www.facebook.com/wandadoolystrange/

Cynthia Tippett serves at The Heights Church in Granbury, Texas on their Dream Team and as a mentor in the Flourish program. She is blessed with an endearing husband, John, two lovable sons, two adorable daughters-in-law, and six joy-enriching grandchildren. One granddaughter resides in Heaven. Her contributions are dedicated to her parents, both strong and full of grace even with the tragic passing of a daughter. Cynthia, a CPA, works out of her home which is commandeered by their two dogs, Uno and Sophie.

Born Adalia Kamp in1950, Dee Dee made her nickname a lifetime preference. Her parents raised her with high hopes and dreams. The birth of her son, Andy, was the pinnacle of her achievements. She learned through almost losing him she needed God above anyone or anything. She answered the call from her Lord to write her first book, *My Shattered Life,* to give hope to others during life's trials and tribulations.

Author website: https://www.deedeeward.com
Email: Warddeedee33@gmail.com

Amber Whiteaker is an ordained minister, with a passion for teaching biblical truths to anyone who desires to learn and grow in their faith. Amber strives to be a true eshet chayil, the "woman of valor," from Proverbs 31. She is an editor, graphic designer, and aspiring writer. When not freelancing or homeschooling, you can find Amber digging into the Hebraic roots of her faith or snuggling with her husband while watching a rom-com. Connect with Amber and watch for new publications at www.amberwhiteaker.com.

Madison Whiteaker is a young, aspiring author who would rather have his nose in a book than do just about anything else—sleeping included. His favorite author, Andrew Peterson, writer of *The Wingfeather Saga* series, inspires him to tie his writing in with his faith and to never fear being vulnerable with his readers. Madison hopes to become a novelist one day and write faith-filled fiction that brings hope to others.

Vicki Woodson is a Christian writer and entrepreneur who loves to share stories that reflect God's grace and her everyday faith. A devoted mother and grandmother, she finds joy in encouraging others through words that uplift and inspire. Vicki lives in Texas with her cat, Tig, and when she isn't writing or reading a good mystery, she's dreaming up new ways to blend faith, humor, and heart into her next story.

About Radical Women

Owner of Radical Women, Lisa Bell, lives in Granbury, Texas. She retired early in 2023 from her position as an editor for NOW Magazines, LLC, covering two of nine markets. She still offers freelance editing of all types (including developmental editing), interior book design, custom cover creation, and she strives to guide and assist writers in publishing their stories independently or with traditional publishers. Whether fiction or non-fiction, Lisa has experience and knowledge to make a story its best possible version.

Lisa also serves as a coach for two writing groups under the name of Radical Writers. She strives to teach writers the skills of writing so their work becomes the best they can achieve. Through writing groups, individual coaching, editing and more, she takes pride in finished products that rival any book regardless of the publisher.

Lisa has published hundreds of articles and multiple books. To learn more about Lisa, contact her by phone, text, email, or visiting the bylisabell website.

www.bylisabell.com.
lisabell@bylisabell.com
www.texasradicalwriters.com
(817) 269-9066

www.ingramcontent.com/pod-product-compliance
Lightning Source LLC
Chambersburg PA
CBHW060457300726
48975CB00008B/2548